"...of your face. Just leave your eyes uncovered."

I'LL BE HOME

Judy Christenberry

A KISMET® Romance

METEOR PUBLISHING CORPORATION
Bensalem, Pennsylvania

In memory of my father, George Russell, who, like Frank, died too soon and is remembered with love.

JUDY CHRISTENBERRY

Judy Christenberry lives in Plano, Texas, with her two daughters and teaches in nearby Highland Park, both suburbs of Dallas. In addition to her children and writing, she enjoys reading and sports, especially baseball.

Printed in the United States of America.

Other books by Judy Christenberry:

No. 5 *A LITTLE INCONVENIENCE*
No. 27 *GOLDILOCKS*

ONE

Lisa McGregor ran down the stairs to the accompaniment of the howling wind. The storm they'd run into south of Amarillo was gaining strength. She was glad she and Paul had reached their destination.

"Mom?" she called as she got to the bottom of the stairs.

"In the kitchen," her mother returned.

When she entered that room, she sniffed in appreciation. "Mmmm, your broccoli cheese soup."

"I thought it might warm the two of you up. Is Paul still unpacking?" Margaret asked as she dried her hands on a dishtowel.

"Yes. I hope you don't mind my bringing him home for a visit." She studied her mother's face.

"Of course not, dear. Your friends are always welcome."

Lisa gnawed on her bottom lip. She hoped Paul Bellows would become more than a friend, but she wasn't ready to confess that to her mother.

"Paul teaches at your school with you?"

"He's the assistant principal there." Their common background and interests were major reasons she was considering Paul as husband material. That and the fact that he was a nice guy.

"Doesn't he have any family?"

Lisa smiled. Margaret couldn't imagine anyone not wanting to go home for Christmas. "Yes. He's going to spend the second week of vacation with them."

Another reason for Paul's visit was to take her mother's thoughts away from Frank, her husband and Lisa's father. He'd died of a heart attack in November of the year before. Last Christmas had been difficult. Margaret, a home economics teacher, loved to entertain. Lisa hoped Paul's presence would keep her mother occupied.

"Are you doing all right?" Lisa asked, unable to hide her concern.

"Of course, dear. You mustn't worry about me." Margaret turned away, hiding her face from Lisa. "That's a mother's prerogative," she added with a laugh.

"There's nothing to worry about, Mom. I'm fine."

"Well, at least you're showing an interest in men again. Ever since your divorce—"

A loud pounding on the front door interrupted Margaret, much to Lisa's relief. She didn't want to talk about her short-lived marriage that had ended shortly before her father's death. Both were painful memories.

"Who could that be? The storm is really bad," Margaret commented as she hurried to the door.

"Maybe they've closed the roads already," Lisa suggested. When winter storms hit Dalhart in the Texas Panhandle, the flat land allowed deep drifts to build, making the roads impassable.

As Margaret swung open the door, two bundled figures rushed in along with a bitterly cold wind and swirls of snow. She shoved the door closed and turned to greet her unexpected guests.

Lisa watched, mildly curious, until a pair of dark blue eyes stared at her. Even as the man reached up to shove back the hood of his ski jacket, she felt the blood drain from her cheeks. Her eyes closed and she prayed he'd be gone when she opened them again.

"Hello, Lisa, Margaret," his deep voice said.

"Ryan! What a surprise."

Lisa considered her mother's words to be a gross understatement.

"Sorry to drop in without warning, Margaret, but the patrolman said the roads are closed and the motels are full. He suggested the high school gym." Ryan Hall paused, shooting a piercing glance at Lisa before turning back to Margaret. "Could we impose on you instead?"

Margaret reached for his jacket and turned to his companion. "Of course you'll stay here."

"This is Erin Steward," Ryan said as a beautiful blonde emerged from the fox-trimmed hood and coat. He assisted her with it and handed it to Margaret's waiting hands.

He'd always had exquisite manners, Lisa remembered. Her lips tightened in irritation.

"Come closer to the fire. It'll take the chill off," Margaret insisted. "Lisa, why don't you bring everyone a bowl of soup? We can all eat around the fire."

The look Margaret sent her daughter was one she'd seen many times before. Do your duty, it said, no matter what you feel. And she would, of course, because her mother asked her. With a nod, she turned to leave the room.

"Call Paul down to join us," Margaret added.

"Yes, Mom," Lisa agreed, relieved to find her voice still worked. Before she faced that man again, she'd make sure her knees stopped trembling, too.

What a delightful evening she had to look forward to. Paul, her mother, herself, the blond beauty, and Ryan— her ex-husand. Oh, joy.

Ryan watched Lisa's hasty retreat. Her white cheeks had told him how she felt about his arrival. She clearly didn't want him here or understand why he'd come. Hell, he wasn't sure himself.

Extending his hands toward the fire, he fought to ignore his reaction to her. Other women were more beautiful, but Lisa, with her red-brown curls falling down her back, her hazel eyes that seemed to look right through you, and a curvaceous body, always set him afire as no one else could.

"It's very kind of you to take us in," Erin said quietly.

"Nonsense. We're used to this happening. Besides, Ryan is—is no stranger."

He grimaced at her wording. No, he was no stranger. He'd been a member of their family for two short months.

In fact, he'd come to Dalhart to talk to Lisa's father, Frank. He and Frank had become friends during his marriage to Lisa, and he'd always found it easy to talk to him. He wanted to ask his advice about his stubborn daughter.

Just as he started to ask where Frank was, the door opened and Lisa entered, accompanied by a man.

Lisa emerged from the kitchen with a full tray just as Paul reached the bottom of the stairs.

"That sure smells good. Let me carry the tray for you."

Lisa surrendered her burden to his stronger arms.

"Five bowls? Has your family expanded?" he asked, giving Lisa a quizzical smile.

He was even-tempered and unflappable, traits that made him a good teacher and administrator. And also good husband material Lisa had already decided.

"The highway patrol has closed the road out of town and we've taken in a couple who's been stranded." She didn't bother explaining just how well she knew one of their guests. With any luck, the storm would end tonight and they'd be on their way tomorrow.

She opened the door for Paul and then followed him in.

"Where would you like me to put the tray, Margaret?" he asked.

"Right here on the table. Shame on Lisa for putting you to work your first evening here," Margaret said as she swept aside the magazines on top of the large square coffee table.

"She didn't. I volunteered. I'd do a lot more for a bowl of this stuff. It smells terrific."

"Thank you. Let me introduce the latest arrivals." Margaret performed the introductions, and the two men shook hands.

Lisa couldn't help but compare Paul's blond openness to the frown on Ryan's dark brow. The last weeks of their marriage, it seemed he was always frowning. Only when they'd been in bed—her thoughts screeched to a halt. That was the last thing she needed to think about.

"Are you cold, dear?" Margaret inquired as she handed Lisa a bowl of soup.

"Why, no, Mom. I'm fine."

"You looked like you were shivering," Margaret added. She reached out to feel Lisa's forehead.

"I'm not sick," Lisa assured her mother patiently. "And your soup would cure me even if I were." She could feel Ryan's gaze on her, but she refused to look his way.

An awkward silence fell before Paul asked, "Where are you folks headed? Colorado?"

Ryan said nothing, but his companion nodded. "Yes. We're going skiing at Vail."

"You've got a long trip still ahead of you," Paul commented.

"Yes. We should've flown." There was a stubborn tone in her voice that told Lisa it wasn't the first time she'd uttered those sentiments. Erin turned to look at Lisa with an expression that lay the fault for their not having flown at her feet. She frowned in surprise.

"I tried to get you to fly instead of driving with me," Ryan muttered.

"Flying's expensive," Paul commented.

"That wasn't the problem." Again Erin looked at Lisa. Before Lisa could question Erin, Ryan disrupted everything with his next question. "Where's Frank? I hope he's not still out in the storm."

Lisa's gaze flew to her mother even as her heart sank. She started to rise, but her mother waved her back into place. "It's all right, honey."

"What's wrong?" Ryan demanded, frowning.

"Frank died of a heart attack November a year ago, Ryan." Margaret didn't look at anyone as her trembling fingers pleated the material of her corduroy skirt.

A painful silence fell, finally broken by Ryan's husky voice. "Margaret, I'm sorry. I didn't know."

Margaret looked up, tears in her eyes. "No. I know."

Lisa jumped to her feet. "If everyone is finished, I'll take the dishes back to the kitchen."

"Need any help?" Paul offered.

"No, I can manage." What she needed help with was getting rid of Ryan and his friend. She gathered the empty bowls as her mother stood.

"I'll go get your rooms ready. Lisa, why don't you move in with me? That way Erin can have a room to herself." Lisa nodded in agreement as Erin expressed her thanks.

"I'm afraid you and Ryan will have to share a room, Paul, since we have only three bedrooms."

"No problem, Margaret. I'm used to being surrounded by hundreds of kids. Ryan won't bother me."

Lisa hoped not. She hoped Ryan and Paul wouldn't spend any time together. Besides, it was Ryan who would be disturbed by such close quarters. In the huge mansion he lived in with his mother, he was never forced to share anything. She couldn't imagine him happy with this arrangement, but he only nodded and expressed his thanks as Erin had.

Erin's attention was caught by Paul's remarks. "You're a teacher?"

"I was, just like Lisa. Now I'm an assistant principal."

His boyish smile didn't resemble the stern image most people had of a disciplinarian.

Lisa noted Ryan's compressed lips, but Erin smiled.

"I bet the girls like being sent to the office at your school."

The teasing smile lit up the young woman's beauty and took Lisa by surprise. To this point Erin had appeared well mannered but disgruntled.

Paul grinned in return. "I'm much meaner than I look."

"Well, if you'll bring in your bags, Ryan," Margaret said, interrupting the conversation, "I'll go make the beds."

Lisa picked up the tray and followed her mother from the room, glad to escape a certain pair of dark blue eyes.

Paul looked at Ryan after the door had closed. "I gather you already knew Lisa and Margaret."

"Yes." He stood and reached for his coat. He had no desire to discuss his personal life with a stranger.

The other man seemed to accept his reticence. "Need some help with the bags?"

"There's no need for both of us to freeze."

"I don't mind. Let me just run upstairs and get my coat." With another grin, Paul left the room.

Ryan zipped up his coat but kept his gaze on Erin, who still stared at the door. "Don't get any ideas."

She turned her head sharply to stare at him. "I won't. I'm here to protect you, remember? I promised your mother."

"And I told you that was foolishness on Mother's part. You saw how Lisa reacted to my presence. If it were left up to her, we'd be camping out in the school gym."

Erin grinned. "It must be a real change for you—a woman who's indifferent to you."

"You mean a woman who's indifferent to my money," he growled. He didn't have many illusions about the female sex.

Paul's return ended their conversation, and the two men dashed out into the storm. The blowing snow stung their faces and made it almost impossible to see. Ryan unlocked the trunk with hands shaking from the cold in spite of his thick gloves. They each grabbed two bags and hurried back toward the light shining in the dark storm.

Once they were inside, with the door closed against the snow and wind, Paul sighed. "I think the storm is getting worse. I could hardly see your car even when I was standing next to it."

"You're right. I'd hate to be out driving in that."

"Do you think it will end by morning?" Erin asked, standing by the fire.

"No," Ryan replied. "But don't worry. You brought enough clothes no matter how long the stay."

Erin grinned, unaffected by his teasing. "You promised not to mention that anymore."

At Paul's raised eyebrows, Ryan explained, "Three of those bags are Erin's. Only one belongs to me."

"Ah. A woman who's prepared for anything."

Lisa interrupted an admiring exchange of looks between Erin and Paul as she came in the den. "Erin, if you'll come with me, I'll show you to your room." Without waiting for a reply, she turned on her heels and walked out. Erin raised her eyebrows but followed silently.

Paul frowned, staring at the door. He almost spoke to Ryan, but he shook his head. He finally said, "Let's carry the bags up and I'll show you our room."

Ryan didn't tell him he already knew which room he'd be sharing. Nor did he tell him he'd prefer another room and another roommate.

They mounted the stairs with the heavy bags and turned to the left at the top of the stairs. The women's voices led them to the first open door. Paul set his load down in relief. "You must've packed the kitchen sink, Erin. These bags weigh a ton."

Ryan added the third bag to the stack but said nothing.

His gaze met Lisa's for a brief look before she turned away. This room had poignant memories for both of them. They spent several days with her parents during their brief marriage. His gaze moved to the bed they'd enthusiastically shared.

"Paul," Lisa called sharply after casting a warning look at Ryan, "would you show Ryan where he's to sleep?"

"Sure. This way, Ryan."

The two men left the room, but Ryan couldn't resist one last look at the room where he'd enjoyed such brief happiness.

Lisa turned away from the two men. "If you need anything, just let me know," she said stiffly to Erin.

"Thank you. You're very kind." As Lisa turned to leave, Erin asked, "Do you think the storm will end tonight?"

Lisa turned back, shrugging her shoulders. "Who knows? We can only hope."

And pray, beg, plead, whatever it took. Lisa slipped into her mother's bedroom and leaned against the closed door. What terrible coincidence had brought Ryan to her door just when she was trying to get on with her life? She hugged her waist with both arms, unable to hold back a moan. One look at that man had done more to arouse her than hours spent with Paul.

That path led to self-destruction, she reminded herself. She'd already traveled it once. To do so again would be masochistic. She could build a good life with Paul, a sensible life, a happy one. She must hold on to that thought— and pray that the storm would end tonight.

She washed her face and went down to the kitchen, where her mother was preparing dinner.

"Are you all right?" Margaret asked softly.

"Sure, Mom. Besides, what choice did we have? I wouldn't wish the school gym on anyone." She sought a change of subject. "Do we have enough supplies to feed all of us?"

"Of course. The freezer is full."

Lisa smiled. Her father used to tease her mother about how quickly she could fill a freezer. "Good. What can I do to help?"

"Set the table. Then you can set the condiments out. We're having pot roast. There'll be plenty. I'd planned on making sandwiches tomorrow with the leftovers," she added with a shrug.

The table was round with six chairs, set by a window that looked out over the backyard. The curtains were drawn now, shutting out the raging storm. As Lisa followed her mother's directions, Erin appeared in the doorway. "May I help?"

Lisa gave a curt no even as her mother said yes. The two women looked at each other, and Lisa's cheeks reddened. In response to her mother's silent reproof, she smiled stiffly at Erin. "You can get the napkins if you like. They're in the pantry."

Erin crossed the room and Margaret smiled at Lisa. She didn't deserve her mother's approval, Lisa thought. But Margaret was right, as usual. Erin wasn't responsible for her anger with Ryan. In fact, Lisa was quite surprised that Erin would even think to offer her assistance. She felt sure Erin came from the same wealthy, privileged background as Ryan.

The three women worked without conversation until Margaret sent Lisa to summon the men. She called Paul when she reached the top of the stairs. When he opened the door, she added, "Dinner's ready."

As she turned to go down, Paul said, "Ryan wanted to ask you about something."

Lisa paused and Paul moved past her down the stairs. Ryan emerged from the room and came toward her.

He'd changed to jeans and a blue sweater that reflected his eyes. His rugged handsomeness was only enhanced by the slight disorder of his dark hair. He'd never bothered with hair spray, she remembered. Her mouth grew dry as he came closer.

"Yes? You had a question?" She stood poised on the top step, ready to run away from him.

"Not really. I just wanted to tell you how sorry I was to hear of Frank's death. And ask why you didn't let me know." There was a hint of anger mixed with regret in his blue eyes.

"It—it had nothing to do with you," she muttered.

"We were friends!"

Her eyes filled with tears and she turned to go down without a word. His big hand closed around her arm.

"Lisa, I really am sorry. But you should've told me."

She knew. Her mother had suggested she tell Ryan when her father died, but she couldn't. The longing to feel his arms around her, comforting her, had been too great. At that moment, she needed to be strong for her mother and herself. She couldn't deal with both losses at once.

Pulling out of his grasp, she gave a brief nod and ran down the stairs.

She heard his footsteps behind her and hurried ahead. The kitchen, with the others, represented a haven for her. Her mother studied first her and then the man behind her as they entered, but Lisa moved to the table.

"Shall we sit down?" she asked, grasping the back of the chair next to her mother's customary seat. She gestured for Paul to sit on the other side of her. It would be impossible to eat if she had to constantly rub elbows with Ryan.

He sat down on her mother's right side after seating Erin next to Paul. Passing the dishes around the table took the place of conversation for the first few minutes.

Once everyone had settled into their meal, Paul asked, "Are you originally from Dalhart, Ryan?"

With a surprised look on his face, Ryan said, "No, I'm from Dallas."

"Oh. I thought perhaps you'd grown up here since you knew Lisa's father."

Lisa held her breath. She didn't want to explain her connection to Ryan. At least not right now.

Margaret intervened. "Ryan met us while visiting friends. He and Frank just took to each other at once." She smiled at Ryan.

Ryan reached out and touched her mother's hand as it rested on the table. Lisa looked away and desperately sought another topic.

"Have you skied a lot, Erin?" she asked abruptly.

"Yes. Most of my life. I love it," Erin replied, smiling.

"Me, too," Paul enthused. "How long are you going to stay?"

"A week. At least, that was the plan." She shot Ryan a sideways look, which he ignored.

"Too bad you couldn't fly. I saw the weather last night and this storm didn't make it that far north. You'd have had good weather for skiing in Vail." Paul took a bite of roast beef.

Lisa, scarcely eating, was struck by his words. Just why had Ryan and Erin decided to drive to Colorado? The weather report had made it clear a storm was coming to the Panhandle. Of course, they'd been wrong about its timing and its strength, but she knew better than Paul that Ryan could afford a plane ticket around the world without blinking an eye, much less one to Colorado. She stared at her former husband.

"Just why didn't you fly?" she asked. "After all, it's a long drive."

Ryan stared at his place and said nothing.

Lisa persisted. "Were the flights already full?"

When Ryan still didn't respond, Erin spoke up. "Oh, it's no accident. We had plane reservations, but Ryan canceled them. We drove so he could stop by here on the way to Colorado."

TWO

All eyes centered on Ryan. When he finally responded, it was to Margaret he looked. "I just wanted to see you and Frank. That's all. I hope it hasn't inconvenienced you."

Margaret smiled and patted his hand just as he'd done hers. "Of course it hasn't. I'm glad you came, though I'm sorry your ski trip is messed up. I caught a weather report on the radio while you were unpacking."

Everyone leaned forward.

"I'm afraid it's not good news. They think the storm will go on for several more days."

Erin groaned, but the two men remained silent. Lisa dropped her gaze, wondering what she'd done to deserve such a difficult situation.

Ryan finally asked, "Do we have enough supplies? Is there anything we need to do?"

"Nothing urgent. There's plenty of food. And I filled the two kerosene lamps and stacked plenty of wood in the shed yesterday."

"You mean we could lose the electricity?" Erin asked.

"Yes, we usually do in a storm like this. At night, the

wind dies down some and the snow builds up on the wires. The weight of it causes them to snap.''

Lisa took pity on Erin's nervous look. "Don't worry. The kitchen stove is gas and the fireplace puts out a lot of heat. We'll all just sleep in the den if it happens.''

"Like a slumber party when we were little," Erin said, giving Lisa a grateful smile.

"Right." A slumber party with one man she thought she wanted to marry and another man who drove her crazy. Lisa kept her gaze focused on her plate.

"We left the gas heater hooked up in the hall bathroom upstairs, too, and the water heater is gas." Margaret added. "We're close enough to be connected to the city water lines. That way, if the electricity goes out, we can still take showers and baths without catching pneumonia.''

"There'll just be a long line," Ryan said. "Of course, we could conserve time and water if we—'' He raised one eyebrow and looked at Lisa.

Red flooded her cheeks. He was doing it on purpose! How dare he remind her of the times they'd shared a shower, and the way they'd always finished it. She glared at him.

"My goodness," Margaret exclaimed, "if you and Paul want to, I suppose you could share a shower, Ryan. I didn't think your taste would've changed so much since the last time I saw you.''

Lisa enjoyed Ryan's red cheeks. Her mother had neatly turned the tables on him.

"All right, Margaret, I'll behave. You know Paul wasn't who I had in mind.''

"I know, dear," Margaret agreed with a smile. "But I'm the chaperone here. You'll have to mind your p's and q's. After all, teachers are experts at chaperoning.''

Lisa jumped up from the table and carried her plate, still half full, over to the sink. "Shall I serve dessert, Mom?" she asked.

"Yes, I suppose everyone is ready for it." She started to get up to clear the table but Ryan stopped her.

"You keep your seat, Margaret. We'll clear the table. After all, you did the cooking."

She settled back down, an appreciative smile on her face.

Lisa couldn't hold back a nod of approval when Ryan looked her way. He always was considerate of her parents.

"I don't mind sharing the duties," Paul said, standing also, "as long as Margaret continues to do the cooking. That was a terrific meal."

Erin brought her dishes to the sink and started to rinse them, but Lisa took them from her. "You can cut the cake if you'd like, Erin, and I'll do this."

"What can I do to help?" Paul asked.

"There's ice cream to go on top of the cake. You can help Erin serve it," Margaret suggested.

Ryan didn't bother to ask for a duty. He stood next to Lisa and took the dishes from her hands, loading them in the dishwasher. Every time his fingers touched hers, she had to make a special effort not to drop a dish.

"You missed a spot."

She stared into his dark blue eyes and forgot what he'd just said. "What?"

He handed the plate back to her. "There's a spot on this one. Do you want to rinse it again?"

"The dishwasher will get it out," she assured him, refusing to take the plate back. She was having enough difficulty passing them to him once.

By the time the other two had fixed the dessert, Lisa and Ryan had finished all but the pots and pans. They joined the others at the table for brownie cake, warmed in the microwave, topped with vanilla ice cream.

"We might as well eat the ice cream right away. If the heating goes, we won't want anything cold to eat," Margaret said. Lisa could tell she was mentally reviewing her menus.

"Don't worry, Mom. We'll eat whatever you put on the table."

The others immediately agreed. Food wasn't what worried Lisa. It was time that weighed on her mind. How would they pass the time? She didn't want to spend any more of it with Ryan than she had to.

As if thinking on her wavelength, Paul said, "There's a bowl game on television tonight. Could we watch it?"

"Might as well while the television is working. I don't think there's anything else on except the hundredth rerun of "Rudolph the Red-Nosed Reindeer.""

"I know which one Lisa would vote for," Ryan muttered, staring at her.

Of course, he knew. She had always been ridiculously sentimental. And she'd never gotten excited about football. Just to confound him, she said sweetly, "Football, of course. I can't wait to see the game."

"Really? Your tastes have certainly changed."

"Yes. Paul still coaches our junior varsity football team. He's explained it all to me."

Erin looked at Paul. "Could you explain it to me? I still don't understand it. And I was a cheerleader!"

Of course she was a cheerleader, Lisa thought. Erin was the epitome of a cheerleader with her blond good looks and bright smile.

"Sure. I'll be glad to. It's easy to understand once someone explains it to you." Always the teacher, Paul enjoyed the opportunity to explain something he loved. When he'd worked at describing the game to Lisa, she'd enjoyed his enthusiasm as much as his explanations.

"Come on. I'll turn on the television for you. Then I'm going to see if Mom needs any help for tomorrow." Anything to stay out of the same room with Ryan. Especially when the other two would be involved in their own conversation.

Lisa led the way into the den, a large room filled with comfortable furniture, and flipped on the television. Luckily, the game was on the channel from Amarillo. The reception for the others wasn't too good.

When Lisa returned to the kitchen, her mother was at the table writing down the changes in her menus. She was always completely organized in the kitchen.

"Everyone watching the game?" she asked as Lisa sat down beside her.

"Yes. It just started."

"I really don't need any help, dear. In fact, I'm just about through. Why don't you go watch the game with the others?"

Lisa rolled her eyes. "You know I don't like football, Mom. Besides, I'd rather—rather stay here with you."

Margaret gave Lisa a sheepish look. "But I was going upstairs to have a bath while the others were busy and then go to bed with a good book I started this afternoon. There's nothing you can do here."

"Go ahead. I'll read this magazine," Lisa said, reaching for a women's magazine lying on a nearby shelf. "Then, at halftime, I'll pop some popcorn for everyone."

"All right. I'll be upstairs if you need me." Margaret gave her daughter a kiss, put her papers on the cabinet, and left the kitchen.

Lisa lethargically turned the pages of the magazine, ignoring the tantalizing titles about sex, love, marriage, and recipes. She couldn't stop thinking about Ryan's arrival. Why would he go to such lengths to visit her parents? What was his reason?

The opportunity to ask that question came unexpectedly when she looked up to discover Ryan standing in front of the swinging door, staring at her.

"Is it halftime?" she asked rapidly, breathing as if she'd broken into a dead run.

"No. I thought you wanted to see the game."

"I—I'm not interested in these teams."

"Oh? Just what teams do you watch?" There was a challenge in his eyes that told her he didn't believe her.

"Texas Tech, of course, and—and SMU. Some of our students have gone to SMU." She didn't want him to think she watched SMU because he was an alumnus of the prestigious private college in Dallas.

He sat down at the table across from her, and Lisa drew a deep breath, trying to calm her racing pulse. He stared at her and she looked away.

"How are you doing, Lisa?"

Her gaze came back to his. She resented the question. They hadn't talked since the divorce. Why this sudden concern now? "Why are you here, Ryan?" she demanded, instead of answering his question.

"I wanted to visit your folks, like I said."

"Now? A year and a half after our divorce? That's a little strange, isn't it?"

"I've been busy," he replied with a shrug. "And I wanted to know how you were doing, too."

"There are easier ways to check on me than driving this far out of your way."

"It wasn't out of the way. And I figured you'd be here for Christmas." He clasped his hands on the table and stared at them. "Is your Mom doing all right since your dad's death?"

Lisa looked away, her throat tightening. She should be able to talk about her father's death without crying. After all, it had been more than a year. But that year had been so difficult, with her divorce and then her father's death. "Yes," she whispered, "yes, she's fine. It's just—difficult for her."

"And for you."

She sank her teeth into her bottom lip. The last thing she needed right now was his sympathy. "We're both fine."

"You know if you or your mother need anything, I'd be glad to—"

"No!" She brought herself under control. "No. We don't need anything."

"Especially from me?" he asked bitterly. "You never needed anything from me, did you? You wouldn't take anything from me while we were married, or after it, either."

Lisa felt as if he'd slapped her. "We were married only two months. There was no reason to take money from you just because we—we made a mistake."

"And while we were married? You didn't want any gifts from me, remember?"

"I remember that you didn't think what I had was adequate. My car, my clothes, jewelry, everything had to be brought up to your standards." She glared at him, her anger rising as she thought back to their marriage.

"What are you talking about?" Ryan demanded. "I bought you those things because I thought you'd enjoy them. It had nothing to do with not approving of you. I married you, didn't I?"

"Yes, because I was good in bed!" she returned.

"But I didn't have to marry you to have you in my bed, did I?" he asked softly, staring as her cheeks flooded with color.

Lisa jumped up from the table. She didn't want to think about those two weeks they'd dated, if you could call it that. For the first time in her life, she'd been swept off her feet. It didn't even occur to her to say no to Ryan. With every other man she'd dated, she'd set limits. Frankly, she'd had no difficulty sticking to those limits either. But everything was different with Ryan.

"I said I'd make popcorn for halftime. Would you check on the game?"

He rose and followed her to the pantry door, and Lisa found herself trapped by his muscular body. "I don't care about popcorn, Lisa."

A shiver ran over her as he pressed nearer. He lifted her chin with a finger and then splayed his hand around her neck, his fingers caressing her skin. She stared at him as helplessly as a rabbit mesmerized by its hunter.

Slowly his lips descended to hers, and Lisa found herself lost in him again, as she always had. It took only one touch from this man to set her aflame. The memory of the pain their marriage brought her was all that saved her from complete surrender.

Wrenching her lips from his, she whispered, "Please, Ryan, please don't do this."

He pushed back from the door behind her. "I didn't intend to," he said, his breathing heavy. "I can't seem to be within a mile of you without wanting—"

She didn't need an explanation of what he wanted. It had always been that way for both of them. Clutching the package of microwave popcorn in her hands, she shoved past him. "If you'll go on in, I'll bring the popcorn in a minute."

"Lisa, we've got to talk."

Stubbornly keeping her back to him, she punched the numbers on the microwave with shaking fingers. "No."

"Why not?"

"Because we never—because *that* happens. And I can't risk losing control again." She turned to face him and said fiercely. "Just leave me alone. I'm trying to get on with my life. I don't need any interference from you."

Without waiting for an answer, she moved to the cabinet to get down several bowls for the popcorn. She sensed him still standing there, staring at her. "Would you open a bottle of cola and pour us all a glass? We'll need something to drink with the popcorn."

At first she didn't think he would do as she requested. Ryan had such determination that he never quit on anything he wanted. At least, he hadn't until their marriage ended. But then, he didn't really want that.

She breathed a sigh of relief as he moved back to the pantry. Pulling a tray out of the cabinet, she set the two bowls on it. The beeping of the microwave announced the popcorn was ready, and she opened the package and dumped its contents into the two bowls.

Ryan silently filled four glasses with ice and put them on the tray before pouring cola into each glass. Lisa added napkins and turned to look at him. "Will you carry the tray for me?"

"Yes. But we *will* talk, Lisa, before I leave. You can count on it."

She didn't answer. Leading the way through the swinging door, she promised herself she'd find a way to avoid talking to Ryan Hall, one way or another.

Ryan followed Lisa into the den, his jaw squared with determination. He knew she didn't intend to talk to him. She hadn't wanted to talk when their marriage had ended either. He'd let her get away with it then because he'd been too angry to talk. But not now.

He saw the sharp look Paul sent Lisa's way as they entered. Not that he blamed the man. When he and Lisa were together, he'd never have put up with another man spending time alone with her.

But he had a prior claim that Paul Bellows didn't know about. And he wasn't ready to turn loose. "Anyone for popcorn?" he asked to distract their audience.

"Not after that huge meal," Erin protested.

"Popcorn's not too filling," Paul countered. "I always have to have it when I'm watching football."

"Or at the movies," Lisa added with a grin.

"You know me too well, Lisa," Paul responded. By explanation, he said to the others, "I always buy a big box of popcorn at the movies, even if we've just eaten."

Ryan clenched his teeth at the familiarity in their conversation.

"Do you like going to the movies?" Erin asked.

"I love it," Lisa answered and Paul nodded in agreement.

"But I can't get Lisa to go see any Stephen King movies. She hates horror," Paul added.

"Oh, I love Stephen King. I read all his books. Did you see *Misery*?"

The other three eagerly traded opinions about movies,

leaving Ryan to his thoughts. He'd been surprised to hear Lisa loved movies. They'd never gone to one after their marriage. He remembered now that while they'd dated, they'd seen several movies and she'd said she enjoyed them. After they married, he'd been involved in a big negotiation that doubled the size of his holdings, and he'd had little time to spend with Lisa. He'd promised her he'd make it up to her later. Only later never came.

"What movies do you like, Ryan?" Paul asked.

"I don't make it to the movies much," he muttered.

"I keep telling him he'd better learn to relax or he'll have a coronary before he reaches forty," Erin teased.

"I imagine you can convince him," Paul said, his gaze as much as his words flattering Erin.

"The game's starting again," Lisa inserted. She didn't look as though she was enjoying this conversation any more than the one in the kitchen.

Ryan turned his gaze to the television, but he didn't pay any attention to the passes and tackles. He kept remembering what it had felt like to hold his ex-wife in his arms again.

He'd tried to forget her. After their divorce, his anger had driven him to date frequently. There are a lot of eager women when a man has money and is willing to spend it. For a while, his dates never ended at the front door. But nothing could take the place of what he'd shared with Lisa.

Finally, he'd given up dating. He thought he needed a break from the females of the world. But the hunger he felt every time he thought of Lisa was still there. Several times he'd picked up the phone to call her. He knew her number by heart, but he'd never dialed it.

His gaze traveled over her as she sat staring at the television. But he didn't think she was watching it any more than he was.

That hunger was why he was here. He'd wanted to find

out if he was crazy, or if what they'd shared was still alive. Now he knew.

She'd left the marriage, not him. He still wasn't sure why. The few things she'd said hadn't made sense to him. At first his pride was hurt and he'd refused to even think about what she'd said.

After six months of trying to forget her, he'd tried to remember those angry words. She talked about their not being suited to each other because of their different backgrounds. She talked about her wanting to teach, whereas he wanted her to attend parties. She talked about not loving him anymore.

That hurt. He'd made mistakes. Assuming she wouldn't want to work since it wasn't necessary. Assuming she'd do the things his mother thought were necessary. He had to spend long hours at the office those first few weeks. By the time the merger was accomplished, he'd already lost her.

He might have found answers to those mistakes. But he couldn't make her love him.

"Wow! What a catch! Did you see that?" Paul exclaimed.

"Oh, it was beautiful!" Erin agreed enthusiastically.

Ryan stared at her in surprise. Only last week she'd protested because he was watching a football game. Paul must be some teacher. He looked at Lisa.

She acted as if she were watching a test pattern. The others' enthusiasm hadn't penetrated her thoughts. He wondered just what those thoughts were. Was she regretting what happened in the kitchen? Or wishing, like him, that they'd continued right up the stairs to the closest bed?

His pride had kept him from calling her. But he knew if she looked his way, if she beckoned to him, he'd sweep her into his arms and carry her upstairs. Pride was poor comfort.

THREE

When Lisa awoke the next morning, her mother's side of the big bed was already empty even though it was only eight o'clock. The second thing she noted was the raging storm still blowing outside. With a groan, she slid to a sitting position. Obviously, there would be no escape today.

She clicked on the bedside lamp to be sure the electricity was still on before sliding out of bed and heading for the bathroom. Last night her mother had already been asleep when she came upstairs and she hadn't wanted to wake her. At least she didn't have to stand in line just yet for a shower.

A short while later, dressed in jeans and a bright yellow sweater, chosen to give her spirits a lift, Lisa found her mother in the kitchen.

"Good morning, Lisa. You look cheerful today."

"That's an illusion, Mom. Have you heard a weather report?"

"Yes, they just gave one at eight." She shook her head as Lisa looked at her hopefully. "Sorry. There's no letup in sight."

Lisa ran her fingers through her long auburn hair, left loose this morning. "I can't believe this is happening."

"It's not so bad, dear. After all, Ryan is a gentleman. I think it was nice that he wanted to visit me and Frank."

Suppressing a scream of frustration, Lisa attempted a smile for her mother's sake. Of course he was a gentleman with her mother. She didn't have to worry about his luring her into his bed. That's what Lisa was worried about— not only that he'd succeed but that she'd forget the pain that would follow.

She jumped up from the table. "What's for breakfast?" It was better if she stayed busy.

"I've mixed some pancake batter. That way we can fix breakfast whenever anyone wakes up."

Lisa took the batter from the refrigerator and fixed her breakfast. She returned to the table with a stack of pancakes and a glass of milk.

The cozy contentment she always found in her mother's kitchen disappeared when she heard footsteps on the stairs. Hoping it would be Paul, she watched as the door swung open.

"Good morning," Ryan said. "I hope I'm not too early?"

"Of course not. You know I'm an early riser," Margaret said, beaming at her houseguest. "Come in and sit down. I've got a pot of coffee on and I'll have you some pancakes made in a jiffy."

Lisa concentrated on her food, but her appetite had disappeared.

"Good morning, Lisa," Ryan murmured as he sat down beside her. She could feel his gaze on her.

"Good morning." She took a bite of pancake to avoid having to say anything else.

Margaret bustled around the kitchen, getting Ryan's breakfast. When she returned to the table, she set down a huge pile of pancakes.

"I can't eat that many, Margaret. I wouldn't be able to

get through the door if I did,'' Ryan protested with a laugh.

Lisa covertly studied him as he talked to her mother. His large frame was covered with solid muscle and not an ounce of fat. She looked away before he caught her. It would be better not to remember how lean and sexy he was.

"Here's your coffee, Lisa. I know you like it after you've eaten," Margaret added, setting down two cups of coffee.

She'd hoped to escape the table as soon as she finished her pancakes. Now she'd have to drink her coffee first or appear rude to the others. "Thanks, Mom."

"You drink coffee now?" Ryan asked, his gaze on her.

"Yes."

"She said she has to have something to wake her up before she faces the kids, or they'll take advantage of her," Margaret explained with a chuckle.

"You like teaching?"

Lisa flashed a quick look at him, wondering why he asked the question. She thought she'd explained her desire to teach as one of the problems when their marriage fell apart. It was impossible to read anything in his eyes.

"Yes."

Margaret chided Lisa with her eyes for her short answers. "It's a demanding occupation. You really have to love children to do it for long."

Doggedly finishing her pancakes, Lisa kept her head down and said nothing more. The other two carried on a rambling conversation that covered a myriad of subjects.

When she was about halfway through her coffee, her mother stood up.

"Well, since Lisa is here to fix breakfast for the other two when they come down, I'll go out to the barn and see about Betsy and the chickens."

"No, Mom," Lisa protested, rising. "You stay in. I'll take care of them." She would've volunteered anyway, and the blizzard would be preferable to staying in the kitchen alone with Ryan.

"What? You're going out in this?" Ryan demanded, standing also. "That's crazy. You could get lost and freeze to death." He stared at the two women as if they'd lost their minds.

"No. Frank rigged a rope between the barn and the house for weather like this. I hooked it up yesterday when it started snowing. I just hold on to it and it guides me straight to the barn," Margaret assured him as she turned to the kitchen door.

"Mom, you stay in. I'll take care of Betsy."

"You're not going out in this alone, Lisa. I'm coming with you." Ryan moved over to stand beside her.

Lisa flashed him one look and turned away. "Don't be silly. I can manage by myself. There's no point in all of us going out in the cold."

"Either I go alone, or I go with you," Ryan assured her in a hard voice, "but you're not going out in this by yourself."

She was tempted to send him out by himself. It would serve him right. But poor Betsy, their cow, needed milking, and she was sure Ryan had never milked a cow in his life. "Suit yourself," she muttered ungraciously and pushed past the swinging door.

"Thank you, Ryan," Lisa heard her mother say, underlining her poor behavior. But then, her mother hadn't had to deal with him as she had.

She gathered her coat and gloves and a hat and scarf her mother had knitted for her. When she returned to the kitchen, wearing snow boots, Ryan was already there. Bundled up in his ski jacket, he looked even larger than he normally did. Margaret hurried in with another long knit scarf.

"You'll need this, Ryan. You must cover the lower part of your face. Just leave your eyes uncovered."

Ryan took the scarf from her and turned to Lisa. "You have one?"

"Yes." Did he have to be so protective? After all, she'd managed for a year and a half without him. She swung her scarf around her head and tied it at the back of her neck. Then she pulled her knitted hat down low.

Ryan slung his scarf around his neck, draping it over his face. Lisa shook her head.

He pulled down the scarf. "What's wrong?"

Slipping her own scarf down, she said, "You have to tie it. The wind will blow it away before you've taken two steps. Here, turn around." She moved over beside him and took the ends of the scarf. Turning him away from her, she tied it into a strong knot, before she moved in front of him and pulled the scarf into place.

"Thank you," he said, his voice muffled.

She nodded and stepped back. Even bundled up to his eyeballs, the man was dangerous. Thank goodness it would be cold in the barn so he wouldn't be tempted to linger. She pulled her scarf back in place and led the way to the utility room off the kitchen.

"Here's the bucket, Lisa. Are you sure you want to do this? I could go get my coat—"

"No, Mom. You stay here. We'll be back in a few minutes." Before she opened the door to the howling storm outside, she turned to Ryan. "No matter what happens, don't turn loose of the rope. If you do, you'll be completely lost and I won't be able to find you." He nodded his understanding of the difficulty and she opened the door.

The force of the wind hit them at once, almost sending them reeling. Lisa grabbed the rope connected to the house by a metal clip. It was stiff and icy beneath her glove, but then so was everything else. The snow stung her eyes and she closed them, using the rope as a guide.

The noise of the storm blotted out every other sound. She bowed her head and followed the rope, hoping Ryan was behind her. As she struggled forward, the snow weighed down her boots, making every step difficult. The bucket in her right hand banged against her leg as the wind tossed it about.

The short walk between the two buildings seemed to take forever. When she finally reached the end of the rope, she almost bumped into the wooden building. Her hand felt for the latch that would open the barn. She had to kick back snow to allow the door to open enough to slip inside. Then she reached back for Ryan and pulled him through also.

Slamming the barn door shut behind her, Lisa pulled off the scarf and shook it vigorously and then did the same to her hat. Ryan seemed dazed by their walk.

"Are you all right?" she asked. Though he nodded, she started knocking the snow from his coat and untied his scarf. "Get as much of the snow off as you can. It will keep you from getting cold so fast."

He followed her directions as she stamped her boots and brushed off her jeans. Betsy's loud mooing reminded them of their chores.

"Okay, Betsy, I'm coming," Lisa called. The cow mooed again, anxious to be milked. Lisa pulled her hat down over her ears again and picked up the pail she'd set down.

Ryan followed her over to the Guernsey cow. "You know how to do this?"

"Yes. It used to be one of my chores when I was growing up. Betsy and I go back a long way." She took a three-legged stool off the wall where it hung and set it down beside the cow. After placing the pail under the cow's udder, Lisa pulled off her gloves and put them in her pocket.

"Won't your hands get cold?"

"Not as long as I'm milking. Betsy's as good as an electric blanket." Lisa grasped two of the cow's teats and began sending streams of frothy white milk into the pail.

Ryan stood watching her, seemingly fascinated. Finally, he asked, "Is there anything I can do?"

"Yes. There's a bag of chicken feed in that closet. Fill the bucket that's in there and put the feed in the feeder. Then, when the hens leave their nests to eat, collect the eggs."

He hadn't even noticed the hens in the other end of the small barn. He turned now, hearing an occasional cluck over the sound of the storm. When he'd followed Lisa's instructions about the feed, he moved back and watched the hens reluctantly leave their nests.

Pulling off one glove, he tiptoed over and picked up the first egg, still warm from the hen's body. Suddenly realizing he didn't have anything to put the eggs in, he slid the egg into his pocket. In all, he collected seven eggs. He returned to Lisa's side. The pail was almost filled.

"I found seven. Is that enough?"

"That's about right. We have only six hens and a rooster. That's more than Mom needs. She sells her extra milk and eggs to one of the teachers at school, though she'll probably need all of them as long as the house is full."

"I'll be glad to pay her for the—"

"No!" Lisa spit out, glaring up at him.

"What's wrong?"

"Do you always think you can buy your way? You would insult Mom if you offered to pay her for the milk and eggs."

He stood there, unsure of what to say. She rose and swung the pail of milk from under the cow. Setting it by the door, she turned back to pull down some hay for the animal.

Ryan moved over to help. As they worked together, he asked, "Does my money bother you so much?"

There was no answer. Finally, he stopped and pulled her around to face him. "Answer me, Lisa. You said something last night about my buying you things. Is it because I have more money? Would you have been happier if I'd been poor?''

"No," she finally answered and looked up at him, a stubborn tilt to her chin. "I didn't mind your having money. But money doesn't take the place of—of more important things."

"I know that."

She shook her head. "I don't think you do."

"Lisa, I wouldn't hurt your mother for anything in the world. But I don't want her to suffer hard times because we've forced ourselves on her. Is that so terrible?"

"No," she muttered.

He stared down at her and found himself lost in her hazel eyes. Without conscious thought, his lips came down to brush against hers. Their softness enticed him, as they always did, and he nibbled the curves of her mouth, warming them both. When his arms went around her, pulling her to him, she made no protest. His lips slanted across hers and he deepened their embrace.

He felt Lisa's hands go around his neck and she pressed herself against him. Impatient to feel her, he unzipped his own coat and then hers while he kissed her. As their bodies came closer together, his tongue teased her and his hands slid under her sweater.

The hunger that rose up in him had never found fulfillment since she'd left him. Only Lisa, with her quick smile, her warmth, her love, had made him feel whole. They sank to the straw-covered ground as he ran his fingers over the smooth skin of her back. She moaned, and it almost sent him over the edge. The sounds Lisa made when he took her stirred him as nothing else could.

He lifted his lips to bury them in her neck, the soft skin tempting him, the scent of her freshly washed hair bringing back beloved memories.

"Ryan—" she murmured, and his lips returned to claim hers, the kiss consuming them both. He cushioned her head with one arm. His other hand slid to her stomach beneath the sweater and moved upward. When he took one breast in his hand, Lisa again moaned and pressed her hips against his.

He gently squeezed her breast, feeling its tip harden, wanting to take it into his mouth. His hardness longed for release, and he slid his hand down to her jeans, seeking the buttons that would provide entrance. Totally consumed in what was happening between them, he scarcely noticed when Lisa first pushed away.

She finally pulled her mouth from his and sobbed, "No."

His hands stilled, but he didn't release her from their embrace.

"No, please, Ryan, no. Don't do this."

Those were the same words she'd used last night.

"Lisa," he gasped, "what is it, sweetheart?"

"We can't do this. Paul—"

As if she'd poured a bucket of cold water over him, the heat died. She didn't want him. She wanted another man. Her body might not agree with her, of that he was sure. But her head said something else.

He pulled away from her and stood up. Turning his back on her, he breathed deeply, trying to control his own body. He hadn't wanted to believe that she didn't love him, but he hadn't asked himself why. He didn't want to be vulnerable.

But he was.

He had just discovered what he'd known all along. Lisa was the one woman in the world who could make him forget everything when she was in his arms. She was a necessary part of his happiness. Without her, success meant nothing.

And she wanted Paul.

"Ryan," she whispered at his shoulder.

"What?"

"I'm sorry, but we can't do this. Sex won't change what we both know. It just won't work."

"Go back to the house, Lisa," he growled. He couldn't look at her, or talk to her, now. Later, when he'd gotten control of himself, he could. But not now."

He heard movement behind him, but he didn't turn around. When the door opened and closed, once more shutting out the howling of the storm, he turned and stared at it. In frustration, he rammed his hands in his pockets, only to remember where he'd stored the eggs.

Pulling his hands out, he stared in disgust as egg yolk dripped from his fingers. What a mess. Just like his life.

Liza zipped her coat as she ran to the barn door. As she opened the door, she remembered her scarf and gloves. She pulled on the gloves and moved out into the storm, trying to tie her scarf as she did so. She reached for the rope, and her hand felt nothing but snow. The panic that filled her was quieted as she backed against the barn. She took a deep breath and moved to her right where the rope should be.

When she felt the rope against her arm, she breathed a sigh of relief. Running her glove along the rope, she moved toward the house. Her scarf absorbed the tears that were seeping from her eyes. She couldn't tell the difference between the snow and her tears. Both made it impossible to see.

She burst into the utility room and closed the door quickly behind her. Before she could take off her outer wear, her mother appeared in the doorway.

"Did everything go all right? Where's Ryan?"

"He'll be along in a minute. I—I was getting cold and he told me to come ahead." She hoped her mother would attribute her red eyes to the storm.

"What a dear he is."

Lisa shrugged out of her coat, shivering as she did so. "I—I'm going to get warm," she muttered and hurried through the kitchen, acknowledging the others' greeting with a wave.

She didn't stop in the den to warm by the fire but hurried upstairs to the bedroom she was sharing with her mother. Closing the door, she stripped off her wet clothes and pulled back the covers of the bed to snuggle down beneath them. Wrapped in a tight ball, she took deep breaths and tried not to think about what had happened in the barn.

That didn't work.

She could still feel his hands touching her, his mouth stirring her. It was as if she was once more the inexperienced girl who became a passionate woman in his arms.

It wasn't fair.

Why should this one man take her to the heights when they were so incompatible, when there was no future for them? Of course, now there was no future for her and Paul either. She'd invoked her friend's name to convince Ryan to stop, but she knew she'd never be able to marry Paul.

Not after Ryan.

She'd thought she could find the kind of marriage her parents had by marrying someone from a similar background. She'd seen herself and Paul, married, contentedly teaching, raising children. But she would never be able to share Paul's bed without longing for Ryan.

And that wasn't fair to Paul. He was a good man who deserved better than half measures. She'd have to find a way to tell him all she could offer was friendship.

What kind of future did that leave her? A bleak one, she acknowledged before chastising herself. She couldn't sit around all day feeling sorry for herself. So, she'd rearrange her future. She'd teach. Her students would become her children. Perhaps she'd return to Dalhart and teach with her mother. Then she'd be sure never to see Ryan again.

Unless he dropped by on a ski trip, of course. A bitter

laugh broke out. Every five years or so, he might feel the need to check on her. To touch her. And in between, she'd live a sterile existence.

Perhaps she could adopt a child. They allowed single-parent adoption now. A tear rolled down her cheek and she sniffed. She didn't think she wanted so much. Just a happy marriage, children. But it seemed she'd asked for the impossible. There would be no children, no marriage, nothing.

Not without Ryan.

FOUR

Ryan stumbled in the storm, milk slopping over onto his jeans and freezing as he moved. He kept a death grip on the rope and leaned into the strong wind.

After what seemed like an hour, he reached the house and struggled with the door. By the time he got it open, Margaret was there to take the milk from him and pull the door shut.

"My, you must be frozen. Oh, your jeans look like sticks of ice."

"I'm afraid I—I spilled some of the milk, Margaret." He shuddered as he drew deep breaths. "I'm not much of a farmer."

"Nonsense. You did just fine. Where are the eggs?"

He licked his frozen lips and ran a gloved hand over his face. "Uh, I put them in my pockets and then fell down. I'm afraid I smashed them all."

Margaret stared at him in surprise. But she didn't ask any questions, as Ryan feared she would. She just patted his arm. "That's all right, Ryan. You'd better go take a hot shower. And bring those jeans and your coat back down to me. I'll wash them while I can."

He stumbled into the kitchen ahead of Margaret and found Paul and Erin sitting at the table.

"Wow! You look like the abominable snowman," Erin exclaimed.

"Thanks," he muttered. "Where's Lisa?"

"She came through here a few minutes ago looking about the same as you," Paul said. "She said she was going to warm up."

Ryan nodded to them and left the kitchen, too. He checked the den, but Lisa wasn't by the fire. When he reached the top of the stairs, he discovered Margaret's bedroom door closed. He knocked and called Lisa's name, but she didn't answer. Thinking she might have fallen asleep, he continued on to the bedroom he shared with Paul. A few minutes later, he was under a hot stream of water and finally beginning to thaw.

When he came back downstairs, Paul was loading the wood bin beside the fireplace.

"Need some help?"

"Nope, I've about finished. This chore is to make up for staying inside where it's nice and warm while you froze your tail off."

Paul's grin was irresistible and Ryan grinned in return. Damn. He didn't want to like the man.

"Has Lisa come down yet?"

"I don't think so. But she might've slipped past me while I was out in the shed. You might check in the kitchen." He bent over to lay a few pieces on the fire.

Ryan continued on to the kitchen. Lisa was sitting at the table with the two other women, drinking a cup of coffee.

"Ryan," Margaret greeted him with a smile. "How about a cup of coffee to warm you up inside?"

"That'd be great, Margaret." He sat down across from Lisa at the round table. "Have you thawed out yet?"

"Just about," she replied but didn't look at him.

"That was kind of you to send her back before you just

because she got cold,'' Margaret said as she sat the coffee mug down in front of Ryan.

His gaze flew to Lisa and she nodded slightly.

"It was nothing. That's a pretty solidly built barn. Did Frank build it?"

"Yes, he did. I helped him, of course. That's how we did everything . . . together,'' Margaret said, her voice ending in a whisper. She cleared her throat. "That's how it should be, you know, in a good marriage.'' She attempted a smile that didn't quite come off.

Lisa reached over to clasp her mother's hand. "You and Dad had a terrific marriage.''

"Now that you're alone, have you thought about moving to Dallas to be near Lisa?'' Ryan asked.

Margaret sat up straight and raised her chin. "Of course not. This is my home. I have my friends and my job. Lisa needs to live her own life.''

Lisa held her tongue, though she intended to discuss her new plans with her mother. But now was not the time. She didn't want Ryan to know she wasn't planning a future with Paul. Not until the storm ended and he was out of her life.

"At least you both have your summers free and two weeks at Christmas. It gives you time to be together,'' Erin added, smiling at her hostess.

"Yes, but Lisa mustn't feel she has to spend all her time with me,'' Margaret said sturdily.

"Of course not, Mom. I'm here because I want to be. And maybe this summer you and I can take a cruise together,'' Lisa improvised. She'd spent most of last summer here with her mother, but she needed to encourage Margaret to try different things. Her mother seemed to be still caught in the mourning they'd both experienced the past year.

There was a welcome spark of excitement in Margaret's eyes. "A cruise? I always wanted to go on one of those, but Frank was afraid he'd get seasick.''

Ryan seemed to hesitate before saying, "I have a friend who works for a cruise line. I bet he could get you a good deal on one. I'll check on it when I get back to Dallas and call you."

Lisa frowned. Things were moving just a little too quickly, and she didn't want any more connections with Ryan after the storm dissipated. "That's okay. We haven't made up our minds yet."

"No problem. I'll just get the information."

"Really, it's not necessary, Ryan."

"What would it hurt, honey?" Margaret asked, puzzled. "Ryan said he'd just get the information." She turned to him. "If you can send me some brochures, I'll get a lot of pleasure just looking at them. And if Lisa is too busy to go, there are a couple of other widows at the high school who might want to try a cruise."

Lisa said nothing else, ignoring Ryan's superior look. At least she wouldn't be here to hear Ryan's praises sung when he sent them. If he sent them. After all, he was a very busy man.

That wasn't fair, she admitted. Even though he'd been extremely busy after their wedding, he'd always kept his promises. He'd just forgotten to listen, or to even ask what she wanted. His mother explained everything to Lisa, Ryan's wants, Ryan's needs, Ryan's feelings.

At first, she'd thought Mrs. Hall was misleading her. But when she tried to question Ryan, either he was too tired to discuss whatever was bothering her or he was more interested in making love to her.

She closed her eyes at the thought. She'd best shy away from that memory. When she opened her eyes, she discovered Ryan staring at her.

"Have a headache?"

"No. I was just thinking." She hoped he'd ignore her red cheeks.

"About something we can do today, I hope," Erin said

with a sigh. "I've never experienced cabin fever before, but I think I have a bad case of it coming on."

"It hasn't even been twenty-four hours," Ryan chided.

Lisa looked up in surprise. That short a time? She felt as if she'd been fighting her emotions for days.

"I know. But just the idea that we can't leave makes me want to race out into the storm," Erin complained, resting her chin in her hand.

"You'd change your mind after about two seconds," Ryan told her. "It's rough out there."

"How about decorating the Christmas tree?" Lisa said, interrupting their chatter. "You were waiting until we got here, weren't you, Mom? Is it in the shed?"

"Yes. I thought—well, it's no fun for just one person."

"Great. We'll decorate the Christmas tree this afternoon. We can make popcorn strings. How about that, Erin? Will that take your mind off the storm?" *And keep everyone occupied,* Lisa hoped. She didn't want any more tête-à-têtes with Ryan.

"Sure," she agreed, smiling. "I didn't mean to complain. That will be fun."

Erin had to make an effort to sound enthusiastic, but Lisa appreciated her trying. This unexpected stopover couldn't be any more fun for Erin than it was for her. After all, if Erin was in love with Ryan, it must hurt her to visit his ex-wife. If she knew.

Lisa jumped up from the table. She didn't want to think anymore. "Mom, why don't you start popping corn, and I'll find some needles and lots of thread."

"What can we do?" Ryan asked, standing.

"You and Paul can bring in the tree. Is the stand in the garage, Mom?"

"Yes. Your father always hung it up on the wall so we could find it the next year. He was a very organized man." Margaret smiled wanly at her daughter.

"Yes, he was," she agreed, squeezing her mother's shoulder. "Erin, will you help Mom?"

"Sure."

They all set about their tasks. Lisa felt better for having something to do. It took her mind off her troubles.

In half an hour, the evergreen tree stood in its traditional corner in the den, waiting to be adorned, filling the room with its pine scent. Margaret and Erin brought in four large bowls of popcorn, and Lisa started handing out needles with long double threads to everyone.

"Even us?" Ryan asked, surprised. "I'm not very handy with a needle."

"This isn't brain surgery," Lisa assured him. "You just stick the needle through the center of the popcorn and push it down the string. Then we'll tie all the strings together and circle them around the tree. It makes the tree look really festive. And after Christmas, we put the tree outside and the birds feed off the popcorn."

"Oh, well, as long as the birds enjoy it," he agreed with a grin that made her heart flop over. She swallowed and quickly turned to hand a needle to Paul. Then she sat down as far from Ryan as she could.

"We could all sing Christmas carols while we work," Erin suggested.

No one wanted to join in, much to Erin's irritation. "Where's your Christmas spirit?" she demanded.

"Some of us just have to concentrate, or we'll be full of holes, like a pincushion," Paul assured her. "And, unfortunately, I'm one of those who can't carry a tune. When they have the faculty choir, they never invite me to participate. Right, Lisa?"

"I'm afraid that's true, Erin. We make him wear the Santa costume."

"Do you like teaching?" Erin asked both of them, a serious look on her face.

"Yes," they answered simultaneously, then laughed.

Paul continued. "Yes. If you don't like it, there's not much reason to put yourself through such agony. But there are those rare moments when you get through to a kid. I guess that's what keeps teachers going.''

"And Lisa?'' Ryan asked. "Is that what keeps you going?''

She studied the popcorn in her hand. "Yes. That and the fact that I believe what I do is important. There's a lot of frustration in teaching. But I know that I can make a difference.''

"Lisa's one of the best teachers we have,'' Paul added, then raised his hand when she would've protested. "No, Lisa, it's true. She's tough on the kids, but by the end of the year, they adore her. They know she's given them her best. It's unusual for a young teacher to be so effective.''

Lisa felt her cheeks flame and kept her gaze on the popcorn. "It's because of Mom and Dad,'' she muttered. "I had great examples to follow.''

"Did you always want to be a teacher?'' Ryan asked.

"Yes. I hardly realized there was anything else.''

Silence fell, but Lisa could still feel Ryan's gaze on her. She wondered what he was thinking. He'd known she intended to teach when they married. But then when he'd planned a trip, a longer honeymoon, for them when his negotiations would be over, she'd explained she couldn't go because school would've started.

That had been the beginning of the end. He'd blown up. She realized now he was on edge, worn out, but at the time, it was the culmination of the neglect she'd felt, the difficulties she'd had with his mother, the fact that they were still living with his mother.

When he'd made no effort to understand the one thing that was so much a part of her, something she'd dedicated her entire college career to prepare for, she thought he cared nothing about *her*, just about his wife. And anyone could've played that role.

"I admire you both,'' Erin said, surprising Lisa. "I think teaching is a very important job. Paul, do you still teach, or do you just do administration work?''

"The coaching is the only teaching I do. But I spend a lot of time with the kids, one on one. And, frankly, for a man who hopes one day to marry and support a family, it's hard to stay a teacher. The salary just isn't that wonderful."

"That's true," Margaret agreed, pushing her needle through another kernel of corn. "I worried about Lisa becoming a teacher. That's why we were glad when she married—that is, when she married a man who could provide some of the nicer things in life," she hurriedly said. "But, of course, that didn't work out."

"I wanted to teach, Mom. It's important to me."

"I know, dear, but once you have children, it's so difficult to do both." Margaret didn't look up from her work. Her fingers were quick and her string was the longest of everyone's.

Children. Her mother didn't know how unlikely it was that she'd ever have any grandchildren. Lisa gnawed on her bottom lip and kept her head down.

"Do you ever need any volunteers at school?" Erin asked.

Paul beamed at her. "You bet. The PTA volunteers do a lot of things in the school. They fix up the teacher workroom, make copies for us, help out in the lunchroom."

"No, I mean, help with the teaching, work with the students." Erin leaned forward, forgetting her string of popcorn.

"Well, we have volunteers who tutor students. Sometimes a company will volunteer an hour a week from their employees. We had a program like that a couple of years ago, before you came, Lisa, but with the tough economic times, they stopped it."

"What did they do?"

"Well, they'd work with a teacher, helping students she'd identified as being particularly needy in a subject the volunteers knew well. Sometimes they'd take the child out of class for one-on-one teaching. Sometimes, they'd assist the teacher in the classroom.''

"That's what I want to do," Erin said.

"You do?" Lisa asked in surprise.

"Yes. I help Mother with a lot of her volunteer work, so I couldn't work full time without putting too heavy a load on her, but I do have some spare time to work at the school.''

"What kind of volunteer work do you and your mother do?" Lisa asked. Mrs. Hall had been heavily involved in volunteer work and had expected Lisa to assist her.

"Oh, a lot of different things. My favorite is a woman's shelter that we solicit donations for. And I answer the hot line a couple of hours a week. It's really sad the problems some people have.''

"Makes the inconvenience of the snowstorm seem minor when you think about that, doesn't it?" Ryan teased gently.

Lisa heard the caring in his voice and it hurt. But she couldn't help but admire Erin. Perhaps she'd been too quick to judge Mrs. Hall. The woman hadn't liked her, but that was no reason to assume her projects were silly.

She stole a glance at Ryan only to find he'd moved over to stand beside her. Ducking her head, she concentrated on the next piece of popcorn.

"Would you want to continue teaching after you had children?"

Her gaze came up to find Ryan staring at her. His question had been asked in a low voice and the others didn't hear him as they continued to chat.

"I—I don't know. My children would come first. It would all depend on whether we needed my salary and how well I could manage.''

He didn't respond and she looked at him again. His face wore a sad expression, one that made him appear older but no less attractive. Turning to look at her, he said softly, "I'm sorry I didn't understand what teaching meant to you, Lisa. I just assumed—I guess I assumed too much.''

She stared into his blue eyes, longing to reach over and touch his face. Maybe they'd both made a lot of mistakes in their brief marriage.

''Ryan, my string is much longer than yours,'' Erin called, sitting down on the sofa on the other side of Lisa. ''You're not working very hard at this.''

The easy grin he offered Erin twisted Lisa's heart. Her time was past. She shouldn't let herself dwell on Ryan and their disaster of a marriage. She stood. ''I'll fix lunch while you all finish here. Then afterward, we'll decorate the tree.''

While Margaret and Erin cleared the kitchen after lunch, Lisa led the two men up the stairs to the attic. The Christmas decorations they used each year were neatly stored in several boxes clearly labeled as to their contents.

Soon they were all in the den and Lisa opened the first of the two boxes. She lifted out a tray of gaily colored balls and set them aside. Beneath were the strings of twinkling lights her father had always strung on the tree first. With a tight feeling in her chest, she offered them to the two men.

''Will you put the lights on for us?''

''Sure you want them?'' Paul asked. ''If the electricity goes, they won't be of much use.''

''When the storm's over, they'll fix the electricity quickly. And we'd have to take all the ornaments off to put them on then.''

''True. I hadn't thought of that.'' He handed a string to Ryan and they each wound the wires around the tree. When they plugged them in, the lights danced all over the tree at random intervals. Margaret directed the replacing of several lights to have them more evenly distributed. When she was satisfied, they were unplugged and the tree looked bare again.

"Well, dear, shall we start putting on the ornaments?" Margaret asked.

Lisa knelt by the box she'd just finished emptying. "Not yet, Mom. The—the star has to go on first." Each Christmas, the first ornament placed on the tree was the big silver star she'd chosen as a very small child. Her father always put it at the top of the tree.

She moved to the second box. "Did you buy icicles for the tree, Mom?" she asked as she began unloading it.

"Yes, of course." Margaret explained to the others, "Lisa always insists on having icicles even though they make a mess."

Erin cheered. "Terrific! I always wanted them when I was little, but my parents said no." She unwrapped a piece of tissue paper to discover a crystal ornament. "Oh, I love this one. It's unique."

"Lisa chose that ornament when she was ten years old. We went to Dallas over Thanksgiving and found a huge Christmas store. It had just about everything you could imagine."

"This one's pretty, too," Paul said, holding up a unicorn delicately painted in pastels.

"That's from the Christmas when she was sixteen. She was quite a romantic then," Margaret explained. "You see, each Christmas, Lisa chose one special ornament. They all hold a lot of memories for us."

"But the most important one is the star," Lisa said as she continued to dig through the box. "Dad—Dad always put it on the tree first. It *has* to go on first."

Everyone else grew silent as Lisa continued to dig through the box. When she reached the bottom of it, she looked up, panic in her eyes. "It's not here! The star's not here!"

FIVE

"Perhaps you overlooked it, dear," Margaret suggested as she got down on her knees beside Lisa on the floor.

"No, I've gone through everything," Lisa said. As she looked up, Ryan saw tears in her eyes. She jumped to her feet. "It must still be in the attic." She ran from the room before anyone could say anything.

"Oh, dear. I hope it's there." Margaret got up more slowly, worry in her eyes.

Ryan stood. "I'll go help her look, Margaret. We'll find it."

He hurried up the stairs, then climbed the ladder to the attic. Lisa was frantically shifting boxes she'd already pulled open to reach others farther back.

"Take it easy, Lisa," he called as he moved toward her.

She sent him a fierce glare. "I've got to find the star. We can't have a Christmas tree without the star."

He tried to help her in her search, but she was like a small whirlwind, frantic to find the important ornament. When she finally slowed down, her shoulders drooped in defeat and tears streamed down her face.

"It's not here. We've lost the star. Just like we lost Daddy," she sobbed.

Ryan stepped over a box and pulled his ex-wife into his arms. "Come on, Lisa. Everything will be all right."

"No. Nothing will ever be right again," she sobbed, burying her face in his sweater. "Nothing."

He sat down on a nearby discarded coffee table and took Lisa onto his lap, his arms wrapped around her. One hand held her close while the other reached up to smooth back her hair, and he murmured soft words of encouragement.

The storm of tears went on for a long time. He suspected they were a buildup of months of missing her father. Lisa had been particularly close to Frank. The star was the culmination of the misery she'd experienced since her father's death.

Ryan wished he'd known about Frank's death, that he'd been able to comfort Lisa, to share her pain. At least he could offer comfort now. A wry smile crossed his lips. This was the first time he'd ever held her without making love to her. It wasn't as satisfying, but it was just as important. He was beginning to realize he hadn't done a very good job of caring for his wife. Maybe he could make up for his neglect just a little.

When the sobs finally stopped, Lisa pushed away from his shoulder, her cheeks flushed. Before she could distance herself too far, he kissed her forehead. "Maybe the star will turn up later on, sweetheart, but whether it does or not, you'll always have your memories of your father. You don't have to have the star to remember how much he loved you."

"No, of course not," Lisa agreed stiffly, sniffing.

"Don't be embarrassed about crying. Everyone needs to cry sometimes." He hugged her and then let her stand. It hurt that she was so anxious to get away from him, even if it was from embarrassment.

"I—I'll just go wash my face and then I'll come back

downstairs.'' She tried a wobbly smile. "We still have a
Christmas tree to decorate.''

"Right. I'll go on down.''

When she reached the attic door, Lisa stopped and
slowly turned to face him again. "Ryan? Thank you for
holding me.''

"My pleasure,'' he assured her, his voice husky with
emotion. He waited until she'd gone down the ladder before he, too, left the attic.

When he reached the den, three pairs of eyes searched
his face for information. "She's okay. We couldn't find
the star, but she's coming down in a minute to help decorate the tree.''

Margaret sighed in relief. "Thanks, Ryan. I wish I
could think what we did with it, but last Christmas is kind
of a blur. It was so soon after Frank's death. Lisa and I
went through the motions, but I don't remember much
about it.''

"That's understandable, Margaret,'' he said, patting her
on the shoulder. "It will probably turn up later on.''

They all sat together, waiting for Lisa to come back
downstairs. The anticipation of decorating the tree had
gone, but Ryan hoped everyone would make an effort to
be cheerful when Lisa appeared. His heart ached for her.

Lisa came down the stairs slowly, not eager to face the
others. She'd lost control of her shaky emotions. At least
only Ryan knew how badly she'd gone to pieces.

It had been such an indulgence to let him hold her, to
cry in his arms. When her father had died, she wanted
Ryan to hold her so badly. But she'd given up any right
to his comfort. It had been for the best, she assured herself, but at the time, and even today, his arms were all
that could comfort her aching heart.

She drew a deep breath before opening the door. As
she entered, she smiled. "Sorry I held us up. I couldn't
find the star, Mom, so I guess we'll just have to decorate

without it." She was speaking too quickly. Drawing another deep breath, she asked, "Have you tied all the popcorn strings together?"

"No, we haven't. Let's see. Who had the longest?" Margaret asked, trying to match her daughter's efforts. "Why, I believe I did. That just goes to show you how much experience counts for. I used to do these strings when I was a little girl." She bustled around tying all the strings together.

"Who wants to put it on the tree?" Lisa asked, before turning to Erin. "How about you, Erin? Have you ever done it before?"

"No. I'd love to. Thanks, Lisa."

Once the garland of popcorn was on the tree, Lisa began passing out some of her own ornaments for the others to place on the tree. She searched for special memories to accompany each one.

When she unwrapped a large lavender heart, Margaret laughed and Lisa's cheeks turned red.

"What's so funny about that one?" Ryan asked.

Giving her mother a speaking look, Lisa said lightly, "I thought I was in love that Christmas. I was seventeen and had a crush on a football player."

"I gather it didn't last," Ryan said, reaching for the heart. "I'll hang it on the tree."

"No, it didn't even last until New Year's," Margaret assured him. "Which was awkward since they'd already made plans for New Year's Eve."

"This is my favorite," Erin exclaimed, holding up a tiny merry-go-round. "Look! They even move."

"Yes, I love that one, too." Lisa unwrapped another and gasped. She closed her eyes and tried to gather her composure.

"What is it, Lisa?" Ryan asked, kneeling beside her.

She couldn't look at him. The sympathy she could hear in his voice would sweep away what little control she had if she looked at him. Raising her hand, she held up an ornament of a miniature dog.

"Dad bought this one for me two years ago. My dog, Butch, died while I was away at school. He looked just like this."

"What a wonderful way to remember him," Erin said softly. "I think your ornament collection is a wonderful idea, Lisa. I'm going to do the same thing when I have children."

Lisa blinked back the moisture and smiled at Erin. "Yes, it is a wonderful idea. Every year I have wonderful memories to cherish. It's like opening gifts I've loved over and over again."

"The only problem is," Paul said, a grin on his face, "as you get older, you're going to have to buy an awfully large tree!"

Everyone laughed at his teasing. Lisa was grateful for their efforts.

"Well, our intention was for Lisa to take her ornaments with her when she set up her own household, so she would have a start on a Christmas tree that would mean a lot to her." Margaret stared at the silver ball in her hands. "When she starts having a family, that's what she'll do."

Lisa didn't look at her mother. The future looked too bleak right now for her to want to think about it. She handed another ornament to Ryan. "Here's a snowflake I bought for the tree this year. It's rather appropriate, don't you think?" she asked, gesturing to the window through which they could see the snow still swirling.

They all stopped to look out at the storm. "At least we're not outside," Ryan muttered.

"Or in the school gymnasium," Erin added, throwing a grateful look to Margaret, while the others chuckled.

Once all the ornaments were hung, Lisa opened the packages of icicles her mother provided. "My favorite part," she exclaimed. Amazingly, after starting out as a disaster, the decorating had become fun. All the memories of Christmases past were healing to her emotions.

"I love this part, too," Erin agreed, coming over to Lisa to receive some of the icicles. Lisa handed some to each of the men, but Margaret declined.

"I'll just watch you put them on." She settled back in her chair and looked at the tree. "Lisa, don't you think we should put something up at the top of the tree since we couldn't find the star?"

Lisa didn't even look at the tree. She knew the top looked bare, but she couldn't stand for anything to take the place of the star. "No, Mom, let's not. We may find the star after all."

"All right, dear."

They began stringing the silver tinsel over the tree. Erin carefully hung one slender icicle at a time. Paul dumped fifteen or twenty strands at once until Erin caught him.

"Paul! You can't do it that way."

"Why not? They all look good together, kind of shiny."

"Because it's supposed to look like real icicles. You hang them one at a time, like this." She demonstrated her technique and the two squabbled over the decorating.

Lisa looked up to find Ryan watching her, a smile on his face.

"They sound like a couple of kids, don't they?" he whispered.

She smiled back. "Yes, but it's kind of fun." She paused, her face turning serious as she awkwardly said, "Ryan, thanks for helping me get through this."

"You would've made it without me. You have a lot of courage."

"Thanks, but—I'm not sure I deserve your support. After all, we're not married anymore."

She watched as his eyes darkened, and she wondered if she'd made him angry.

"No, but we can be friends, can't we?" He watched her, his blue eyes intent.

Friends. What a difficult word. She wanted to be friends with him, but she wanted so much more. She nodded and turned away, hoping he wouldn't see the longing she felt. They'd never really been friends. The sexual attraction had been so strong, so overwhelming, she didn't think they'd really gotten to know each other before their marriage. And afterward, he'd been too busy for them to be friends as well as lovers.

If she couldn't be his lover, perhaps being his friend would suffice.

She was lying, of course.

Once the tree was finished, Margaret served hot chocolate with marshmallows floating on top, and they turned out all the lights except for those blinking on the tree. The crackling of the fire accompanied Christmas music being played on a local radio station.

They sat around the tree in contentment. Lisa stared at the top of it. The missing star was rather symbolic of her life the past year or two. She seemed to have lost her direction.

Surely they'd find the star. And hopefully, she'd find her way also. Ryan reached out and touched her hand, causing her to jump in surprise.

"We never got to have a Christmas together. I'm enjoying this one. I hope you don't mind." He whispered so the others couldn't hear.

"No, I'm enjoying it, too," she told him. "But what about your mother? Is she all alone?" Even Mrs. Hall didn't deserve spending Christmas alone.

"No. She and several friends went on a Christmas cruise. She's enjoying the hot sun and midnight buffets," he added with a wry laugh.

Margaret overheard his words. "And she left you alone

at Christmas?'' Her voice expressed the horror she felt at such behavior.

"I'm not a child anymore, Margaret. Besides, Mother and I had a, uh, falling out, and I imagine she's still angry with me."

Lisa wanted to ask what had caused their argument, but she didn't. She watched as Ryan and Erin exchanged a long look. Had it been about the two of them? Surely Mrs. Hall wouldn't protest a marriage between Erin and Ryan. After all, Erin was everything Lisa was not. And everything Mrs. Hall wanted.

Nothing about Lisa had pleased her mother-in-law. She'd wanted a debutante, well connected, with a fortune of her own. She'd wanted someone who wore designer clothes, drove an expensive car, and dined only at the best places. Instead, she'd gotten Lisa, who sometimes wore homemade outfits and preferred jeans, liked fast food, and drove a Chevrolet.

Mrs. Hall had made her displeasure clear.

Lisa shook her head. She didn't want to think about her ex–mother-in-law. "I'm glad she's enjoying herself," she murmured, before adding, to change the subject, "Are there any Christmas specials on television tonight? I'm not in the mood for more football."

"There's a Hallmark special on," Margaret said eagerly. "I've been looking forward to it. I hope the electricity stays on so we can watch it."

Just then the music on the radio stopped and a newscaster's voice came on. "We interrupt this program for the latest weather bulletin. The storm currently engulfing the Panhandle is predicted to continue for at least another twenty-four hours. Accumulation is expected to be two feet or more with drifts of up to eight feet. The low tonight will be minus two degrees with the high tomorrow expected to reach eight. Please remain indoors and take the proper precautions."

Paul stood up. "That calls for another log on the fire.

Just thinking about how cold that is sends shivers up my spine.'' He moved over to add a piece of wood to the flames.

''If the electricity goes out, will your pipes freeze?'' Ryan asked Margaret.

''Well, Frank insulated them really well, so I hope not. Do you think we have enough wood in the shed to last us several days?'' She looked at the two men for an answer.

''We'll go out and check, Margaret. We'd better plan on three days just to be sure. We'll work out a rationing of it so we won't run out.'' Ryan motioned for Paul to follow him, and the two men left the room.

''If we have to, we can always burn some of the things I've stored in the attic. It needs a good cleaning out,'' Margaret muttered to herself.

''It won't come to that, Mom,'' Lisa assured her mother. ''What's for dinner? I'm getting hungry.''

The three women adjourned to the kitchen to fix the meal.

The next morning, when Lisa woke, she was glad she'd taken her shower the night before. Her breath hung in the air above the bed, a frosty white.

The electricity was gone.

She sighed and considered staying in bed, snug under the covers. Sometime during the night, her mother must've risen and added to the blankets on the bed. There was a satisfying comfort to the weight of quilts on a cold morning.

The thought of her mother already downstairs, probably preparing breakfast for all of them, was enough to nudge Lisa's conscience. She threw back the covers and raced for the bathroom. The sooner she got dressed and downstairs, the sooner she'd be warm again.

The fire was burning briskly in the fireplace in the den when she peeped in there, but Lisa continued on down the hall. She pushed open the door to the kitchen.

"Brrr! I think I've turned into an icicle," she complained as she greeted her mother.

"Sit down and I'll bring you a cup of coffee to warm you up. It has to be instant since the percolator is electric, though."

"That's all right. As long as it's hot."

Before she got her cup of coffee, the two men entered the kitchen. Margaret immediately filled two more cups and carried all three to the table.

"How come it's so warm in here?" Paul asked, rubbing his arms.

"I've had the gas burners on the stove on for over an hour and the oven turned on." She gestured to the open door of the oven. "It puts out a lot of heat."

"The den's not too bad either, with that big fireplace," Ryan said. "It's just the upstairs that feels like the North Pole."

"I laid out some of Frank's long underwear for the two of you. It might be a good idea to put it on under your clothes," Margaret suggested. "Lisa has her own, but she'll share with Erin."

The last member of their group rushed into the kitchen. "I'm f-frozen," Erin complained, shivering.

"Where's your coat?" Ryan asked.

"I didn't think to wear it to breakfast," she snapped back.

"Temper, temper," Paul teased.

Lisa stood up and went to the utility room door. Reaching past the door, she pulled a coat from the hook on the wall and then closed the door behind her.

"Here, Erin. Throw this around your shoulders until you warm up. Mom will fix you some coffee and you'll be warm in no time."

Erin threw her a grateful look before glaring again at her traveling companion. "Lisa's a lot more sympathetic than you are."

"I told you she's a nice person."

Lisa stared at the two of them. His words were a surprise. When he'd first arrived, she would've sworn he'd blacken her name at every opportunity. Now it appeared she was wrong. But there seemed to be some significance to what they were saying beyond the teasing.

"You're right." Erin sipped her coffee, avoiding Lisa's gaze.

"Have you heard a weather report this morning, Mom?" Lisa asked, deciding a change of subject might be a good idea.

"More of the same. This is the worst storm since 1968, they said."

"I'm glad your stove is gas," Paul said. "At least we won't have to cook over the fire. That rather limits the menu."

"But it might be fun," Erin added. "Kind of romantic."

Paul chuckled. "That's not what I consider to be romantic. I like my food too much." He leaned toward Erin with a mock leer on his face. "What I consider romantic is cuddling together to keep warm. I figure I've got it made, as cold as it is."

"In your dreams!" Erin exclaimed, returning his grin.

"Oh, yeah? Well, maybe I'll cuddle with Lisa instead and leave you to freeze."

"Then I'll cuddle with Ryan and Margaret. With three of us, we'll be warmer than you."

Lisa studied her coffee cup. The thought of cuddling with Ryan to stay warm, or for any other reason, warmed her all over. She sneaked a look at his face and found him staring at her, a small smile on his lips. Was he thinking the same thing? Her cheeks flamed at the thought.

"Well, I thought we'd have bacon and eggs for breakfast this morning," Margaret said, interrupting their teasing. "I have enough eggs without anyone collecting them before breakfast. Afterward, I'll need them for cooking, of course, and Betsy has to be milked. Lisa, will you and Ryan—"

"No!" two voices exclaimed.

SIX

A startled silence settled over the five people. Margaret cleared her throat.

"Well, I can go take care of things," she said, avoiding looking at anyone.

"No, Mom, that wasn't—" Lisa hurried to explain.

"No way, Margaret. I can—" Ryan protested at the same time.

Ryan and Lisa broke off their protests and looked at each other. Lisa wasn't sure what she saw in his eyes, but his rejection of being alone with her hurt. Of course, she'd rejected the same idea. Because she couldn't trust herself.

"I meant there's no need for two of us to get wet and cold," Lisa said before Ryan could speak again. "I'll go by myself."

"Wrong," Ryan said briefly, his features stern and unrelenting, like his response.

Her head snapped up and she glared at him. "I beg your pardon?"

"I'll be the one to go." He didn't speak as if she had an option, but Lisa wouldn't allow him to dictate her behavior in her own home.

"Oh, yeah?" she replied, sarcasm lacing her words.

"Betsy would really appreciate that. You don't know how to milk a cow."

Ryan stood. "I watched you yesterday. It didn't look too hard."

"Listen, Ryan," Lisa protested, rising also.

"Is this a private argument, or can I join in?" Paul asked calmly.

"It's private," Ryan said with steel in his voice. He glared at the other man as if he'd challenged him.

"I was just going to suggest," Paul continued as if Ryan hadn't spoken, "that I go with Ryan to the barn. I *do* know how to milk a cow. In fact, I could go by myself and—"

"Fine, we'll both go." Ryan's tone left no room for argument.

Even so, Lisa didn't like the high-handed way he'd behaved. "I don't see why you're being so difficult."

Erin touched Lisa's arm. "They're both being gentlemen, Lisa. I think we should encourage them instead of discourage them."

"You're right, Erin," Margaret agreed. "Now, both of you go upstairs and put on the long underwear I left outside your bedroom door while I fix breakfast." As they turned to go, Margaret added, "And Ryan, try not to break the eggs this time."

He gave her a reluctant grin before his gaze continued on to Lisa. "That won't be a problem *this time*, Margaret."

"What did he mean by that?" Erin asked after the door had swung to behind the men.

Lisa felt the other two staring at her, but she shrugged her shoulders and hoped her cheeks weren't red. "He probably means he'll be more careful this time."

"I hope so or we'll be reduced to oatmeal for breakfast, and you know how much you hate oatmeal," Margaret reminded her.

The frown on Margaret's forehead told Lisa she was already working out an alternative menu. "Mom, quit worrying about the food. If the storm doesn't end soon, I'm going to put on five pounds because you're feeding us so well."

"Oh, I know," Erin groaned. "I've eaten more since we got here than I normally do in a week."

"You don't have anything to worry about," Lisa said with a rueful smile.

Erin stared at her as if making a decision. Instead of thanking her for the compliment, she finally said, "You know, Lisa, you're quite a surprise."

"I am?"

"Mildred Hall told me all about you."

Lisa's brows arched and her smile grew stiff. Ryan's mother wouldn't have had anything good to say about her. "I see."

"Yes, I can tell that you do. But I've discovered that she was wrong. You're not at all what she described."

"Well, thanks for that, Erin. I didn't know whether you knew about—that is, that Ryan and I—"

"Were married?" Erin grinned. "Oh, yeah, I know."

Lisa looked at her mother and then Erin. "Paul doesn't. I think it might be better if we don't mention it while we're all trapped—uh, staying here."

Erin blinked several times and then smiled ruefully. "Right. I'll try not to spill the beans."

"It is hard," Margaret chimed in from the kitchen counter, where she was beating eggs. "I almost did earlier when we were talking about teaching."

"There's no need to make a federal case out of it. If it comes out, it's no big deal," Lisa said, tracing the duck pattern on her coffee mug.

"You and Paul are—" Erin didn't finish her statement, letting it hang in the air as she stared at Lisa.

"Good friends."

Lisa's succinct response ended all conversation for several minutes. Then, Erin tried again.

"You're dating?"

Lisa didn't hesitate. Anything she told Erin would go straight to Ryan, she was sure. "Yes."

"Ah. Well, he's a nice guy."

"Yes, he is," Lisa agreed as the door swung open and the two men came back into the kitchen with their jackets on their arms.

"I feel about as graceful as the Pillsbury Dough Boy," Paul complained, sticking his arms straight out and waddling over to the table. Erin broke into laughter.

She reached out to poke him in the middle. "I think you're a little thicker than him."

"Watch it, young lady, or I'll make *you* go to the barn with me," he threatened.

She slanted her head back and stared up at him, asking in a sexy drawl, "Is that a threat or a promise?"

As if only then realizing what she'd said, Erin shot a guilty look at Lisa and hurriedly said, "I was just teasing, you know. Sometimes I speak without thinking."

Lisa took pity on her embarrassment. "That's easy to do with Paul. He teases a lot."

"Hey, don't blame it on me," Paul returned, but his gaze had never left Erin's red cheeks. "I'm an innocent."

Margaret carried a plate of scrambled eggs and another of bacon and sausage over to the table. "Come on. Sit down and eat before everything gets cold. Lisa, will you get the toast? Oh, and Erin, pour the orange juice in those glasses I set out."

Soon everyone was enjoying Margaret's fluffy eggs.

"If we don't leave soon," Ryan said a few minutes later, interrupting Erin and Paul's joking with his hard voice, "we'll get too hot." He shoved back from the table and stood. "That was a great breakfast, Margaret. Thanks."

Paul frowned at the irritation in the other man's voice but nodded in agreement. "Right. Is the milk pail in the utility room, Margaret?"

"Yes. I'll—"

"I'll get it for them, Mom," Lisa said, rising from the table. She led the way into the utility room and found the pail, giving it to Paul.

"You understand how important it is not to let go of the rope?" she asked both of them. They nodded, and she swung open the door to the fury of the storm. Paul slipped through the opening.

Ryan pushed the door closed, much to Lisa's surprise. Without a word, he reached out and pulled her against him, his lips covering hers in a searing kiss that left her knees shaky.

"W-what are you doing?"

"Rewarding myself for not taking you to the barn this morning." With that cryptic remark, he pulled open the door and disappeared into the storm.

When Ryan reached the barn, Paul had already taken the milking stool off the rack on the barn wall. He turned as the door closed behind Ryan.

"I was afraid you'd gotten lost. That's a pretty strong storm out there."

"No, I just stopped to talk to Lisa a minute." He watched Paul warily approach the cow. "You're sure you know how to do this?"

Paul smiled. "I've milked a cow before, but it was only once, and I didn't consider it to be a satisfying experience for either one of us."

"Then why did you volunteer for this duty?"

Paul turned his back on Ryan and placed the stool beside the cow. He sat down on it before looking over his shoulder. "Because I was afraid you and Lisa were going to come to blows."

"I just didn't want her out in this storm again," Ryan protested defensively.

"Yeah." He looked down at his gloved hands and then at the cow's udder.

Ryan answered his unspoken question. "Lisa took hers off."

"I was afraid of that," he said with a sigh.

"You want me to do it?"

"No. I bragged about being experienced. Now I have to pay the price. You try to improve your record with the eggs."

Without responding to Paul's teasing, Ryan fetched the chicken feed and filled the bin for the chickens. There was less hesitation this morning as they flocked to the feeder. He gingerly searched the nests for the eggs, finding nine this time. Again, he placed them in his pockets.

When he returned to the other end of the barn, Paul was gradually filling the bucket with milk, though not with the speed Lisa had exhibited.

"Not bad," Ryan said with a grin. "You've convinced me of your experience."

"I'm not sure I've been as persuasive with Betsy," Paul said wryly. "It took us a while to get started."

Ryan watched in silence, waiting for him to finish.

Paul, with his head tucked down against the cow's flank, suddenly asked, "You and Erin been dating long?"

"What?" Ryan asked in reflex.

"I said have you—"

"I heard what you said. No." *Why did he want to know?* Ryan wondered. *The man was here as Lisa's guest. How could he even think about another woman?*

"But you've known each other a while?"

Ryan glared at Paul's unsuspecting back. "Yes."

Paul caught a remnant of the frown as he looked over his shoulder. "And you'd rather I stop asking questions?"

"Yes."

"I wasn't trying to cut in on your territory," Paul muttered. "The lady's out of my league. But she's—nice."

Ryan tried to hold back his anger. After all, it wasn't Paul's fault that he found Erin attractive. These things just happened. Look at him and Lisa.

He hadn't intended to fall in love when he went to his cousin's graduation. But Lisa McGregor took his hand and he suddenly knew he didn't ever want to let go. It had taken him a while after the debacle of their marriage, a year and a half to be exact, but he knew now his first instinct was the right one.

All he had to do was convince Lisa. She seemed to think they were incompatible. He wasn't sure why. He hadn't been understanding about her teaching, but he knew better now. Her happiness was more important than anything else.

But he sensed that there was more to it than just her teaching. And he mustn't forget the last thing she named in her list of complaints. She said she didn't love him anymore.

He'd believed her at the time. He'd believed her until yesterday morning in the barn. Lisa didn't have a lying bone in her body. If you didn't want to know her honest opinion, you'd best not ask her a question. And she couldn't let him be passionate with her as she did yesterday without feeling something for him.

He'd realized that last night as he'd tried to get to sleep. She hadn't accused him of assaulting her, forcing himself on her. Even more, she'd responded. So much so that he almost lost control.

It was her words afterward that haunted him. She saw sex as a problem, not a solution. That's why he couldn't let himself come to the barn with her this morning. He wasn't sure his self-control would allow him to be alone with her without touching her. Until he figured out what went wrong, he was going to have to find some self-control.

"Ryan?"

He jerked up his head and stared at Paul standing before him, a quizzical look on his face.

"At first I thought you were ignoring me because you were mad at me. Then I realized I could've shoved you out in the storm and you wouldn't have noticed." His grin faded and he asked, "Is everything all right?"

Ryan shook himself, trying to pull himself together. "Yeah, everything is fine."

"I promise to keep my hands off Erin."

There was a teasing challenge in Paul's eyes that Ryan couldn't help reacting to. "As if I'd consider you a threat," he scoffed, punching Paul on the shoulder in typical male fashion.

Grinning, Paul punched back and then turned to the barn door. "Let's get back to the house before this long underwear freezes to my skin."

"I'm right behind you."

"What are we going to do today?" Erin asked, sounding dispirited now that the three women were alone.

"Cabin fever again?" Lisa asked.

"Yeah, and we don't have a tree to decorate today."

"We could always take it down and start over, one icicle at a time," Lisa teased.

Erin blushed. "You and Paul are the biggest teases. But I enjoyed decorating the tree. You know, usually Christmas is so rushed, I don't have time to really enjoy the important things. There are so many parties and activities that when Christmas is over, I just feel relieved."

"Now we don't have a choice but to slow down," Lisa agreed. "When I was growing up, Mom and Dad made Christmas special because we were all off for two weeks."

"What else did you do for Christmas?"

"Oh, we usually cut down our own Christmas tree." She looked out the kitchen window at the solid white storm. "I guess that's not an option." She paused to think of Christmases past. "We always made Christmas cookies. Mom would put them in tins and give them to our neighbors for Christmas presents."

"Decorated cookies, like stars and trees?" Erin demanded, her eyes lighting up.

"Oh, yes," Margaret assured Erin. "I have some really nice cookie cutters. One is in the shape of a little church with a steeple. Then there's a stocking, a candy cane, Santa, a present, and, of course, a bell, a star, and a Christmas tree."

"What fun. Have you already made them this year?"

Lisa and Margaret exchanged looks. Finally, Margaret said, "No, I haven't. We—we didn't make them last year, what with everything that happened, and I hadn't even thought of it this year. It's so late, I'm not sure—"

"Oh, I wasn't trying to talk you into it," Erin protested. "It just—just sounded like fun."

"If we all pitch in, Mom, I bet we could do them all in one afternoon. We could start baking now and decorate after lunch."

Margaret sat there thinking, and Lisa crossed her fingers under the table. The more things returned to normal for her mother, the better she would be. And the more activity she could keep everyone involved in, the less she had to worry about Ryan.

"You're right. There are a lot of people I need to thank for their help this past year. I'd like to make our Christmas cookies again. It will be a big job. Are you sure you want to do it?"

Both young ladies assured her of their support.

"But what about Paul and Ryan? Do you think they'll want to help?"

"We're sure they'll want to eat them, and we can convince them to help," Erin replied, grinning.

Lisa was sure Erin was right. As lovely as she was, neither man would be able to resist her. She studied her fingers twisted in her lap. At least this time Ryan had chosen someone well suited to be his wife.

"Lisa? Is anything wrong?" Erin asked.

She looked up to find both ladies' eyes on her. "No. Of course not. What shall we do first, Mom?"

"I'll start mixing a large batch of dough. You dig out

the cookie cutters and rinse them off. Erin, get the wax paper out of that second drawer and cover the table with it. Then—'' She had her troops working hard within a matter of minutes, energized by the project.

When the men came in from the storm, Margaret met them at the utility door and helped them brush off the snow. She took the pail of milk from Paul and looked at Ryan expectantly. ''Did the eggs arrive safely this time?''

''All safe and sound in my pocket, Margaret.'' He followed her into the kitchen and unloaded his pockets, putting the eggs on the counter.

''Good job, Ryan,'' Margaret said, smiling at him. ''While you're still dressed warmly, why don't you and Paul go ahead and bring in enough wood to last us until tomorrow morning, if you don't mind. We'll need to keep the fire burning all night, don't forget.''

They came through the kitchen with several loads of wood, staring at the goings-on as they passed by. After they finished the last load and cleaned up, they both came to the kitchen and looked inside.

''What's going on here?'' Paul asked.

''We're making Christmas cookies,'' Erin explained as she pressed down on a cookie cutter. She had a streak of flour on one cheek, and she was wearing one of Margaret's aprons.

''I didn't know you could cook, Erin,'' Ryan teased, but his eyes were on Lisa. She smoothed down the arpon she wore and hoped she, too, hadn't decorated herself with flour.

''I'm full of surprises. Besides, who could go wrong with Lisa and Margaret to guide them?'' She held up her latest creation, a cookie cut in the shape of a church. ''Isn't this just darling?''

''What is it?'' Paul asked.

''Really! Can't you see? It's a little country church. I'd like to be married in one like this,'' Erin said dreamily, studying the cookie shape.

Lisa's eyes flashed to Ryan. The church in which they'd been married had resembled the one in Erin's hand. It was a short distance from Lubbock and had been the only one available on such short notice. Ryan had brought her a beautiful bouquet and a corsage for her mother. He and her father had worn boutonnieres.

The look in his eyes told Lisa he was remembering also. Tears gathered unexpectedly as she turned away. It had been a beautiful wedding, simple but beautiful. Mrs. Hall had often lamented the lack of pomp and circumstance, and even more about her own absence, but Lisa had treasured her memory of that little country church.

"Somehow I can't see you marrying in a simple little church like that," Paul said dryly.

Erin frowned. "Why not?"

"From what you've said, your family has money and position in Dallas. People like that have these big, elaborate weddings with a thousand guests and a catering bill that would feed me for five years."

There was a tinge of bitterness in his voice that surprised Lisa. Paul never seemed to mind doing without things that others considered important.

"Not necessarily. Ryan didn't."

Lisa held her breath and kept her gaze on the dough on the table.

Paul paused before saying, "I didn't realize you were married, Ryan."

"I'm not," he snapped. "I'm divorced."

Lisa cut out another star and laid the dough shape on the cookie sheet lying on the table. If she concentrated on her task hard enough, perhaps no one would notice her flaming cheeks and shaking hands.

"It doesn't matter where you are married," Margaret said serenely from over by the cabinet. "Frank and I were married before a justice of the peace, and our marriage lasted thirty-eight years. And they were wonderful years."

"My parents were married in a big ceremony, with a

huge catering bill," Erin added with a pointed look at Paul, "but their marriage has lasted almost thirty years. And they're very happy. I think Margaret's right. It's not where you're married that matters."

"It does to whoever is paying the bills," Paul muttered, gripping the back of a chair tightly.

Erin stared at him, her eyes reflecting her irritation. "Don't you believe in love?"

"Of course I do."

"It's hard to tell," Erin said.

Lisa looked up at Ryan, not surprised to find his gaze on her. "I think what matters most is that you come from similar backgrounds, share the same interests. *That's* the most important thing."

Ryan stared at her, the look in his eyes unreadable. "Are you sure, Lisa?"

SEVEN

"Good gracious, all this deep discussion over a poor little cookie," Margaret exclaimed, saving Lisa from having to respond. "You boys go in the den and read or something while we finish making the cookies. Then, after lunch, we need you to help us decorate them."

"Yes, ma'am," Paul said with a mock salute. As they turned to go, he muttered to Ryan, "I feel like I'm seven years old again."

Ryan laughed but his eyes were still serious as he looked back over his shoulder at Lisa. He'd seemed surprised at her words, which puzzled her. She'd told him, at the end of their marriage, that they weren't alike. Why would he be surprised?"

"I think you've made enough stars for a while, dear," Margaret said softly. "Why don't you switch to bells?"

Lisa looked down at all the stars she'd fiercely cut out and grimaced at her mother. "I guess you're right. I'd better pay attention to what I'm doing."

Erin gathered up scraps of dough left from her batch and began to pat them into another ball to be rolled out. "Working with dough is so satisfying, isn't it? I'd love to learn to make bread."

"If we're stuck here long enough, I'll teach you, Erin," Margaret promised.

Erin beamed at Margaret, but Lisa could only hope and pray baking bread didn't become necessary. She was counting on an earlier release from their white prison.

After lunch, Margaret mixed icing in the four basic colors and settled the others around the kitchen table with piles of cookies waiting to be decorated.

"Aren't you going to decorate, too?" Ryan asked.

"No. I'm going to clean the kitchen and put on a pot of stew for this evening. I'll leave the creative part to you four."

Lisa leaned over the table in a mock confidential manner. "She doesn't really like the decorating part. She always tried to convince me she was saving the best part for me. It took me a while to figure out what was going on."

"Now, Lisa—" Margaret protested, a smile on her face.

"It's true."

"Well, I'm delighted to do this," Erin said, reaching for one of the church cookies. She examined the tools Margaret had put out, her cake decorating utensils along with knives and icing, tiny silver balls for decoration, and colored sugar flakes. Like a surgeon choosing a scalpel, she made her selection and began to work with a serious look on her face.

Lisa passed the plate of cookies to the two men, encouraging them to take more than just one. "After the first four or five, you won't be quite so particular about how it's done. At least I hope not. We've got about five hundred cookies to decorate."

Paul began a mental calculation in his head. "That's over a hundred cookies apiece."

Ryan cocked one eyebrow. "Maybe we should eat a few to lower the numbers."

"We saved the brown cookies for you to eat," Erin said even though she didn't look up from her task.

"Oh, sure, that's all we get, the burned ones," Paul protested.

Lisa watched Erin work, fascinated. She'd taken white icing and covered the body of the church. Blue icing went on the roof, and now she was using yellow icing to form a tiny window and door, as if light were pouring forth in the dark night. Then she took the tiny silver balls and outlined the roof with them, putting each one at a precise distance from the others.

"Erin, that's beautiful," she praised. "Mom, come look."

Margaret moved over to the table. "Oh, my, Erin, you have quite a talent."

Flushed with pleasure, Erin gave a modest response, even as the men joined in the praise.

"However," Ryan added, "if you take that much time with each cookie, we'll be here until New Year's."

"Spoilsport," Erin muttered.

"You just keep on making cookies like that one, dear. We'll let the others do the fast work. Then, when we pack the tins, we'll put one of your special cookies on top."

Erin was pleased with Margaret's solution, and the other three good-naturedly worked at speed. Margaret puttered around the kitchen as they worked, providing cups of coffee at intervals. The stacks of decorated cookies grew until they began to have difficulty finding places for all of them.

"Oh, dear, I think it's time we bring down the tins."

"You already have them, Mom?" Lisa asked in surprise.

"Yes, I bought them just before—early last November. Then we didn't do the cookies last year. They're stored in the attic."

"I'll go bring them down," Lisa said, relieved to get away from decorating more cookies. She always enjoyed the first dozen or two, but then the decorating got old.

She was up and out the door when she heard her mother

send Ryan after her. It was too late to protest since she was already in the hall. She tried anyway.

"I can manage on my own," she said as he came through the door.

"No, you can't."

"How do you know?" she asked, irritated.

"Because I need an excuse to get away from those blasted cookies, too."

His grin reached right into her heart, and she couldn't help but respond with her own. "It does get old, doesn't it? I used to do almost that same amount by myself. Sometimes Dad would help for a while, and Mother would do some, but that was one chore at Christmas that I got tired of."

"Unlike Paul and Erin. I guess we have more in common than you think," he added as he took her arm and encouraged her down the hall, away from the others.

"I don't think not liking to decorate hundreds of cookies is a significant trait," she said dryly, starting up the stairs.

"No, but getting bored with routine is. And wanting to do your best at what you do is another. Being passionate about your work, wanting to help others, enjoying laughter, all those seem important to me." He pulled her to a halt at the top of the stairs.

The air was much colder there, but that didn't account for the chills Lisa felt. "We—we don't have that much in common." She avoided his stare.

"Those things don't describe you?" he asked gently, reaching out to take hold of her arms and pull her closer to him.

"Maybe, but there are other things," she hurriedly said, her eyes wide as she watched him.

"Yes, there are. Making love in the early morning, when the house is quiet and we're in a world of our own. Touching you even when we're in public, just to feel you next to me. Watching you dress, brush your hair, even read a book. Those are things I enjoyed."

"Stop it, Ryan," she whispered. "We aren't married anymore. We just agreed to be friends." Her gaze dropped down to his chest. She couldn't look into those deep blue eyes any longer without losing herself completely. "Anyway, what about coming from different backgrounds, wanting different things?"

"Different backgrounds only affect the surface, Lisa. They gave each of us something different to contribute to our marriage."

"Right," she agreed sarcastically, trying to fight the emotions that were swamping her. "Only it didn't work out that way, did it?" She tugged at his hold, trying to pull away.

As if her movement incited him, he pulled her closer to him. When he lowered his head, she knew she should protest, but the hunger that filled her couldn't be denied. Instead, her mouth opened to his, and she didn't resist as he pressed her body against his.

His warmth, the sound of his racing heart, the always remembered scent of him, part male, part after-shave, enveloped Lisa, and her hands slid up his broad chest, reaching for the warm skin of his neck, the silk of his dark hair. He tightened his hold on her, pressing her breasts against his hard chest.

She longed to feel his hands on her, feel his flesh against hers. As if reading her thoughts, one of his hands slid beneath her sweater to caress her back. His tongue sought entrance to her mouth, and she welcomed it with her own. She was consumed with wanting him, just as she'd always been.

His mouth left hers to rain kisses all over her face before descending to her neck. His nibbles sent chills down her body. She thrust her hips against his, eager to feel the hardness she knew was waiting for her.

When his lips returned to hers, he also slid an arm beneath her hips and lifted her inches from the floor. Intent on what his mouth was doing, Lisa was barely aware of their movement. When she realized they'd entered her bedroom, it seemed only right.

Ryan laid her down on the bed, and she reached eagerly for him, needing his warmth, his wanting, him, to fill the aching void in her body, her life. When he joined her, his mouth returning to hers, his hands slid up her sweater, exposing her breasts, still captured in a lacy bra, to his look.

She moaned as his hands covered her breasts. They ached for his touch. Her own hands tugged at the sweater covering his broad, hairy chest. The shirt beneath the sweater frustrated her, and she pulled at the buttons, ignoring the several that popped off.

Running her fingers through the silky hair on his chest, she exulted in the remembered pleasure. She'd missed him so much. He lifted her to remove her sweater and unclip her bra, and she willingly assisted. Then she demanded equal rights, pulling his sweater and shirt from his body.

Bare chest to bare chest, their kisses deepened, until their breaths mingled as one, as if neither could survive alone. But they weren't yet satisfied.

Ryan's hand slid to her jeans, vying with the buttons for control. Lisa, too, let her hands wander down his strong body, seeking the opening to his jeans. Her body was singing in exultation, like a starving man faced with a banquet. She'd longed for his touch night and day, unable to sleep because she'd dream of him.

When they lay naked together on the bed, ignoring the cold air around them, Ryan suddenly slowed his actions, caressing, touching, savoring her body. Lisa thought she would scream as he held them both back.

"Ryan, please," she whispered before her mouth joined his. She pressed against him, pleading with her body for completion.

He moved over her and settled between her legs, his familiar weight driving Lisa on to greater heights. When he drove himself into her, she seized his shoulders and arced her body to take all of him. Without thought, only the pure knowledge of pleasure long withheld, they moved in unison, bringing each other to the height of pleasure, crashing in ultimate release against each other.

Lisa, her eyes closed, clung to Ryan's body as he lay atop her, enjoying his weight, feeling her bones melt into the bed. She'd thought she would never feel such completion ever again. Now she held on to it as long as she could.

Ryan finally moved, squeezing her tightly against him even as he withdrew from her. His lips nibbled at her neck and he whispered her name.

Slowly she opened her eyes, reluctant to face reality. His blue eyes smiled at her, welcoming her back. A hand reached out to caress her face, and his lips returned to hers. Gently. His tenderness after making love was one of the sweetest parts of Ryan.

He drew her head to his shoulder and cradled her against him, his hands warming her body with his caresses as he rubbed her back, her thighs, her stomach, her breasts. She gasped as he pressed himself against her. Already he was eager for her.

"Again?" she asked hazily, her fingers touching him.

"Always. I never get enough of you," he whispered.

His mouth returned to hers and Lisa was closing her eyes, sinking once again in the warmth of sensations when her gaze was caught by Erin's yellow ski jacket with the fox trim hanging on the back of her door.

The reality she feared set in with a painful harshness. He was no longer her husband. They had no future together. He should've been making love to Erin, not her. She pulled away from him without a word.

"Lisa?"

Ignoring his question, she gathered her belongings, scattered about the floor and bed, and ran from the room, clutching her clothes to her bare chest. She slammed the door to her mother's bedroom behind her and leaned against it, sobs wracking her body.

What had she done?

Damn! Ryan sank back against the pillow, despair filling him. He *knew* he couldn't trust himself alone with her. He'd certainly proven himself right.

Cold began to seep into his skin, reminding him of the storm raging outside. He wearily got off the bed and began searching for his clothing, slipping into them as he found them. He ignored the buttons missing from his shirt. With the sweater on top, no one would know.

But the missing buttons reminded him of another thing he'd proven. Lisa wanted him as much as he wanted her. It also reminded him that wanting wasn't enough. They had to share more than the bedroom. And he was determined to prove to her that they could.

He only hoped she'd let him within a country mile of her after today. Otherwise, he'd have to do all his courting over the telephone—if she didn't slam it down in his ear.

He went to the attic ladder and climbed up, his eyes quickly spying the tins neatly contained in two shopping bags. He thought he'd seen them yesterday. Swinging up one in each hand, he stepped back down the ladder.

Before he went down the stairs, he paused by Margaret's bedroom door. "Lisa?" he called softly. There was no answer, but he was sure this room was where Lisa went. "Are you all right?"

Still no answer.

He wasn't surprised, but he'd hoped she might respond. Shrugging, he continued on down the stairs.

Entering the kitchen, he tried a smile, but he was afraid it might look a little grim if it reflected his state of mind right now.

"Goodness, we thought you two might've gotten lost," Margaret teased. Her smiled faltered when she realized Ryan was alone. "Where's Lisa?"

"She stopped off in your bedroom for a minute," he said, hoping Margaret wouldn't rush right up to see about her only child.

"Oh. Did you have trouble finding the tins?"

Erin and Paul scarcely acknowledged his return, showing no concern for Lisa's absence. He had only Margaret to convince. "Lisa buried them when she was looking for the star yesterday. It took a little while to uncover them."

Distracted, Margaret started lifting tins out of the shopping bags. "Yes, she was upset about the star. I can't imagine what could've happened to it. We're always so careful to store everything neatly. That's Frank for you. He's so careful—" She broke off and then said, "He was always so careful about things like that."

Ryan silently patted Margaret on the shoulder and helped her stack the tins on the cabinet. She surreptitiously wiped her eyes and said. "I need the green tissue paper from the den, Ryan. Would you get it? It's in that box of wrapping paper and ribbon by the television."

"Sure, I'll get it."

"Hey, wait a minute," Paul protested, looking up from the piles of cookies around him. "How come I'm being left to finish all these cookies while Miss Precise Decorator works on her masterpieces?"

"Must be because you're so much more talented than me," Ryan mocked. "All I'm good for is my brawn."

"Or you're just a lot smarter than me, seizing a good opportunity when you see one," Paul muttered. "As soon as you get that paper, I expect some help."

"Yes, sir," Ryan agreed with a grin.

"Oh, and you'd better check the fire while you're in there," Margaret added. "After all, we'll all be sleeping in there this evening. We need to keep the room as warm as we can."

"I think it might be fun, all of us in one room," Erin commented.

"That depends on whether or not you snore," Paul teased.

"I don't! How dare you suggest such a thing?"

"I don't know. I just didn't look forward to being kept awake all night by you sawing logs."

"You're probably the one who'll keep *me* awake. You big football types always snore," Erin returned.

Ryan left the kitchen as Paul replied to her teasing. He knew who would keep him awake all night. To have Lisa in the same room with him, only a few feet from him, and yet be unable to take her in his arms, to cradle her against him as they slept, would drive him insane. It would certainly make sleep impossible.

How could she have any doubts about the rightness of their marriage, of their being together, after what just happened? Didn't she trust her heart?

He moved over to the fire and removed the screen. Reaching for a large log, he laid it carefully on the fire. Picking up the poker, he levered the log into a more secure position and then watched as the flames licked eagerly at the new fuel. He'd been consumed with desire and love as he'd held Lisa in his arms. But he wasn't the only one.

Did she think the desire that exploded between them was only of the flesh? That he wanted her only because she turned him on? That was a part of it, but he'd learned there was much more. He'd slept with other women since his divorce. At first he'd done so frequently, hoping to prove to himself that Lisa wasn't special.

He'd failed.

No matter how beautiful or how willing, none of the women had made him want her as he wanted Lisa. None of the women had evoked the desire to hold her forever, to protect her, to love her. He hadn't wanted any of them to carry his child, a son or a daughter, as he wanted Lisa to. Even thinking about Lisa pregnant sent a shudder through his strong body.

He allowed his imagination free rein, seeing Lisa heavy

with their child, holding a newborn against her full breasts, suckling it. Staring at the Christmas tree, he imagined their own, with special ornaments decorating it and several children surrounding it.

They'd never talked about children. Hell, they'd never talked about anything. He'd come back late at night and taken her to bed. He winced as he remembered a few times when she'd tried to talk to him. It hadn't seemed important at the time when their future hinged on his performance at the conference table the next day.

Now he knew he was paying the price for his careless treatment of Lisa. But he would win her back, he promised himself. He would find a way to convince her of his love, of his resolve to be more careful of the most precious thing in the world to him. He would find a way to hold her in his arms forever.

Sighing, he turned from the tree and found the green tissue paper where Margaret had said it would be. Everything in its place. He grinned. He could use her in his office.

He opened the door to the hallway just as Lisa reached the bottom step of the stairs. They both stopped.

"Lisa—" he began.

She silenced him with a sharp wave of her hand, looking away as if she couldn't bear to see him. "Don't. Don't say anything."

"Lisa, we have to talk."

"That's what you said before," she whispered fiercely, "but that's not what happened, is it?"

"I didn't intend—"

"No. Neither did I." She turned back to stare at him, a hard look in her eyes. "I don't intend to say anything to Erin. You tell her what you think best after you leave here." When he started to speak, she stopped him again. "I don't want you to say anything to Paul, either."

Without waiting for his promise, she walked past him into the kitchen.

EIGHT

Lisa entered the kitchen with Ryan right behind her. She moved around the table, standing just behind Erin.

"It's about time you came back. I need help," Paul protested. "You two aren't doing your share."

"You're right," Lisa agreed, trying to smile. "If you'll scoot over, I'll take your place and you can help Ryan line the tins with tissue paper."

"Why do I need to move?" Paul asked, staring up at her.

Because I can't let Ryan close to me. Afraid for a moment she'd spoken out loud, Lisa scrambled for an answer. "It's just good organization. Decorators over here, tin liners over there."

Erin laughed. "I think you'd better hire Lisa for your company, Ryan. She sounds better qualified than the man you took on last week."

"You're probably right. Want to come to work for me, Lisa?" Ryan asked.

She carefully examined the knife Paul had been using. "No, I don't think so. I want to teach."

"If you did, you might have enough money to get your car repaired," Paul said, grimacing.

"What's wrong with your car?" Ryan snapped.

Lisa said nothing, focusing on the cookie she was decorating. She hoped the others would think it was a matter of artistic concentration.

"Her transmission is about to go out," Paul explained.

"It's still under warranty, Lisa. Take it back to the dealer."

Lisa peeped at the two men from under her lashes and continued to decorate her masterpiece.

"You've got to be kidding!" Paul exclaimed with a laugh. "That clunker? It's at least ten years old."

"What happened to the BMW?" Ryan asked, his voice hard.

"What BMW? Did you own a BMW, Lisa?" Paul asked, confusion in his voice.

"Yes. My ex-husband bought me one." She flashed a warning look at Ryan.

"Nice. He must've been a generous guy. How much tissue paper do we use, Margaret? One sheet or two?"

"Two, and overlap them, Paul. And yes, her ex-husband was a generous man," Margaret added, throwing a reproachful look toward Lisa.

"Or worried about his reputation," Lisa muttered.

"Or even worried about his wife's safety." Ryan stared at her, and she ducked her head.

"So, what did you do with it?" Paul asked.

"I sold it." It had been an act of defiance, she admitted to herself now. Mrs. Hall's rude comments about the car she'd driven had irritated her. Perhaps she'd been wrong to attribute his mother's attitude to Ryan, but he'd never asked her if she wanted a new car. It just appeared one day and her car was towed off. All they did was allow her to take her personal belongings out.

"What are you driving now?"

She didn't want to tell him. But if she didn't, Paul probably would. "A Ford."

"It's not a bad little car, but it needs a tune-up, and

when they get to be that age, there are some repair problems.'' Paul began layering cookies in the tin he'd just lined. ''How many cookies, Margaret?''

''Oh, the number doesn't matter. Just fill it, but leave room on top for one of Erin's special cookies.''

''I know a good mechanic who doesn't charge a lot. When we get back to Dallas, why don't I have him look at your car?'' Ryan asked carefully.

''That's a good idea,'' Erin said unexpectedly. ''I don't care how far we've come as women, Lisa, mechanics just don't take us seriously.''

Lisa was surprised. If *her* man had wanted to help another woman, especially his ex-wife, she might not have encouraged him.

''Thanks, but I'll manage.''

''Do you always have to be so stubborn?'' Ryan asked.

''I have to take care of myself. That's called being an adult, not being stubborn.'' She glared at him.

''Everyone needs help every once in a while,'' Margaret murmured, not looking at her daughter.

''Mrs. Hall lets Ryan take care of everything for her,'' Erin added. ''I guess it's okay since he's her son. He's awfully patient with her.''

Which is probably why he thought he didn't need to consult me either, Lisa admitted to herself. ''Everyone's different,'' she muttered.

''Yeah. Mrs. Hall wouldn't be caught dead in a Ford. You should hear some of her comments when she sees old cars on the street,'' Erin said, rolling her eyes.

''I've heard them,'' Lisa muttered. She could feel Ryan's stare, but she refused to look at him. ''If we hurry, we can finish before dinner, and I'm really hungry tonight. By the way, Mom, have you heard the latest weather report?''

Surely God would answer her prayers soon.

After dinner was eaten and cleared away by the light of

the kerosene lamp, Margaret began organizing their sleeping arrangements. Both sofas in the den made out into queen-sized beds, used frequently when Lisa had real slumber parties as a teenager.

"We three ladies can sleep on one bed and you men on the other. We'll use our sleeping bags as well as extra quilts for cover."

"As long as we keep the fire going all night, it shouldn't get too cold, will it, Margaret?" Ryan asked.

"No, but someone would have to put wood on the fire every couple of hours. Whoever did it wouldn't get a lot of sleep."

Ryan started to volunteer his services since he didn't expect to sleep much anyway, but he just nodded. He didn't want to say anything that would make Lisa more leery of him. She'd been jumpy throughout dinner, keeping as much distance as possible between them.

He didn't blame her for not trusting him. Making love to her instead of talking was a mistake. Visions of their moments upstairs came to him. He couldn't regret it. But it sure as hell complicated what he was trying to do.

"You unhappy with the arrangements?" Paul asked, drawing Ryan from his thoughts.

"What? No, of course not."

"Well, you sighed like the weight of the world was on your shoulders."

"No. I was just thinking of something else." He glanced at his watch. It was only seven o'clock. What were they going to do all evening? Lisa stood over by the window, her shoulders drooping. What was she thinking?

"I know what we can do this evening," Erin said, drawing everyone's attention.

"Well, what's your big brainstorm?" Paul asked. "If it's charades, you can forget it," he said with an amiable growl.

"No, smarty, it's not charades, though that's not a bad idea," she teased.

"Oh, no, you don't."

"Anyway, I want to play Monopoly. Do you have a set, Lisa?"

She had to ask twice before Lisa heard her. When she did, she admitted she did have the game when she was younger. "Is it still here, Mom?"

"Oh, yes, dear, it's up in the attic, on one of the shelves."

"I'll go up and get it." Before anyone else spoke, she added, staring at Ryan, "And I *don't* need any help."

There was silence after Lisa left the room. Finally Erin said, "Do you think Lisa's too tired to play, Margaret?"

"No, dear. She just gets grumpy sometimes."

Ryan noticed Margaret looked at him before she continued spreading a quilt on one of the beds he'd pulled out for her. He knew he was part of the problem, but until he and Lisa got some privacy so they could talk—and nothing else, he promised himself, until they'd worked everything out—he didn't know what to do about it.

Lisa reentered the room clutching a large Monopoly box. "Where shall we play? I think the kitchen might be best."

Everyone agreed and moved toward the door.

"Aren't you coming, Mom?"

"Oh, well, if you don't mind, I think I'll go ahead and get in bed and read. I have a new murder mystery I want to start. And if I'm asleep before you finish, don't worry about waking me. I sleep like a log."

The other four trooped into the kitchen, where the other lamp was still burning on the table. As they sat down, Erin said, "Your mother is so nice. She hasn't complained once about all the work we've caused her."

The two men agreed, but Lisa said, "She's enjoying it. Actually, I think it's helped her. Last year Christmas was rather difficult, you know."

"But she never gets upset about anything. Even when

I burned, I mean, let the cookies get too brown, she just smiled."

"Burned was the right word. I tasted one of those cookies," Paul complained. Erin gave him a disgusted look.

"Teachers are trained to be flexible and unflappable. When you're in charge of a lot of children, if you remain calm, they're more likely to do so," Lisa explained, smiling. "And Mom's been teaching for a long time."

"She's right," Paul said. "Remember that bomb scare last year?"

"You had a bomb scare?" Ryan demanded, a fierce frown on his face. "When was this?"

Paul seemed surprised at his intensity. "I think it was in March. Anyway, we got everyone out of the building, but one of the teachers freaked out, and her class did, too. That kind of thing is catching."

"I thought teaching was safe," Ryan growled.

"About as safe as anything else," Lisa said coolly. She maneuvered herself between Paul and Erin as everyone sat down at the table.

"Teaching must be great training for being a mother," Erin said. "My mother fainted when I skinned my knee. Blood was running down my leg and I looked a mess. Luckily, Dad was home. But I thought I was dying since Mom took it so hard."

"Yeah, Lisa will be a great mother, but I'm sure you will, too," Paul murmured.

Ryan stared at Lisa, and he knew the instant the thought hit her because he realized it at the same time. They hadn't used any protection.

He'd been careful to do so every other time. Even after they were married, he'd wanted some time alone with Lisa before children became a part of their family. But not today. Not today when there was no family.

The thought left Lisa breathless. A child. She could already be carrying Ryan's child. She wrapped her arms around her waist and kept her gaze lowered. It was a secret she intended to share with no one.

"Lisa? Do you want to be the banker?"

"Oh, no, Erin. Someone else would be better. Ryan, perhaps?"

"He's certainly a genius at high finance. He doubled the size of his company a couple of years ago. That was the summer I was in Europe and—" Erin broke off, her guilty look passing from Ryan to Lisa and then to the table. "Anyway, he'll make a good banker."

Ryan reached for the money and deeds and began distributing the paper money, saying nothing.

"Just what kind of business are you in?" Paul asked.

"Electronics, microchips."

"Ah. I've heard that market's hot right now."

It was Erin again who responded. "It is. Ryan's so wealthy, he's considered Dallas's top bachelor. Every woman in Dallas is after him."

"You talk too much, Erin," Ryan said abruptly. "Lisa, do you want to be the top hat or the race car?"

"The race car," she said, just as untalkative.

"I'll bet you had to make a hefty settlement when you got your divorce. After all, Texas is a community property state," Paul speculated, watching Ryan. "Probably makes you leery of remarrying."

The look Ryan shot Paul was not friendly. He held out the dice. "Roll to see who goes first."

Paul reached for the dice. "Sorry, Ryan. I didn't mean to pry."

Lisa felt Ryan's eyes on her as he said, "My wife didn't want any of my money, Paul. She refused any kind of a settlement."

"Wow. She must be some woman, or wealthy herself."

"You were right the first time. Your roll, Erin."

"Anyone want anything to drink?" Lisa asked, jumping up. She needed to do something to change the conversation.

"Why don't you roll the dice before you fix coffee?"

Ryan suggested, holding out the dice to her. "Then we can get the game started."

She rolled the dice and was surprised when they stopped on double sixes.

"Looks like you start first, Lisa. I'll put on water for coffee," Erin said.

Lisa started the game, rolling the dice again.

An hour later, she had collected twelve properties and a lot of cash. Every time she rolled the dice, she got just the number she needed.

"I think I should take you to Las Vegas," Paul suggested after she'd landed on the only unsold property. "You just can't miss tonight."

"I don't think she'd do as well in Las Vegas. She has a phobia about money," Ryan muttered.

Lisa opened her mouth to object but then shut it again. Perhaps Ryan was right. She was uncomfortable with his wealth. She'd just never realized it before. It was easier to blame his mother for everything.

"Aren't you going to roll?" Erin prompted, staring at Lisa.

"What? Oh, yes." She turned the dice loose on the board, scarcely noticing the result. Because Ryan's wealth had made her uncomfortable, she'd rejected every gift he'd given her, perhaps even seeing it as a condemnation of her parents and the way she'd been raised.

While she'd realized Ryan was comfortable, maybe even more than comfortable, when they married, she hadn't really understood the scope of his wealth. And that was before he doubled his operations that summer.

He'd told her and her parents that he had his own company. In Dalhart, that didn't mean immense wealth. They'd just never comprehended his importance. Then, when they'd come to Dallas, Lisa was overwhelmed by the difference in their lives. Without Ryan's support, since he was working twelve to fifteen hours a day, it was left to his mother to help Lisa adjust.

That had been the last thing Mrs. Hall wanted to do.

"Lisa, are you going to buy Park Place or pass on it?" Paul asked. "You've been staring at it for five minutes."

"I'll buy it," she muttered, avoiding Ryan's gaze. He'd stared at her most of the evening.

The game continued on for over three more hours. Lisa thought it'd never end. Finally, Erin was bankrupt. She left the room to get ready for bed, and Paul lost a lot of his enthusiasm for the game.

When he went bankrupt, leaving Ryan and Lisa to fight it out to the bitter end, she abruptly said, "I'm really tired. I don't think I want to play anymore, if you don't mind, Ryan."

"But Lisa," Paul protested, "you've got him beat. If he lands on Boardwalk this round, you'll finish him off."

"Why don't you take my place and finish it, Paul? I just don't have the energy."

"Are you all right?" Paul asked, walking around the table to place a hand on Lisa's forehead. "You haven't seemed like yourself all evening."

She pulled away from his touch, noting Ryan's narrowed gaze, and stood up. "I'm fine. I just don't want to play anymore. Is that all right with you, Ryan?"

"Sure." He started stacking the money and putting the game away. Paul moved to help, along with Lisa.

Erin stuck her head in the door. "Someone else's turn in the bath. Oh, you're finished? Who won?"

Before either man could respond, Lisa said, "No one. We decided to quit. Who wants the bath next?"

"Ladies first," Ryan said, gesturing to the door.

Lisa didn't hesitate. She wanted to avoid any private conversations.

The gas heater in the bathroom kept it cozy, and it and the flashlight Erin had handed her provided enough light to do what was necessary. After collecting clean clothes from her mother's bedroom, Lisa stripped and stepped under the hot shower, grateful her father had installed a gas water heater. They really didn't suffer too much when the electricity went out. There was only the inconvenience of the kerosene lanterns and taking a shower by flashlight.

She giggled. How romantic. Then images of past showers that *had* been romantic sobered her. Best not to think of those. She was growing more and more confused. Blaming Ryan and his mother for the failure of her marriage had been easy. But now she was discovering some things about herself that made such an easy escape impossible.

Her father had warned her not to run away from her marriage and her husband. His advice had hurt. She'd assumed he'd done so because he liked Ryan. Now she realized he'd understood his only daughter better than she'd thought. As much as Ryan had't listened to her, she hadn't listened to him either—or accepted his way of life.

She'd heard of marriages when the husband or wife expected life to go on as before. As silly as she thought that was, she and Ryan had both done exactly the same. They'd each assumed nothing would change.

And instead of fighting for her marriage, she'd run away. Just as her father had said.

"Hey! Don't use all the hot water!"

Lisa almost slipped in the shower. Thankfully recognizing Paul's voice, she immediately shut off the stream of hot water. "Okay. I'll be out in a minute."

She hurriedly dried herself off and pulled on underwear and the soft sweats she'd chosen to sleep in. She added thick socks and then gathered up her discarded clothes and bath towel. The shower cap had almost kept her hair dry. She shook her hair out and ran a comb through it.

"Thanks," Paul said as she opened the door. "I thought I was going to freeze before you came out."

"I didn't know you'd formed a line," she said with a smile.

"Only a line of one. Ryan and I flipped to see who went next. He's down building up the fire."

Good, Lisa thought. That meant she could slip through to the utility room and leave her dirty laundry. Then she could go right to bed in the company of Erin and her mother, safe from any confrontations with Ryan.

"It's all yours," she said, gesturing to the bathroom.

Paul went in past her, and she moved to the top of the stairs. She stood listening for sounds in the darkness, but all was quiet except for the wind still blowing outside. Avoiding the third stair that creaked, she tiptoed down to the hallway. The door to the den was closed to keep in the heat. It also allowed her to pass through the kitchen to the utility room without anyone seeing her.

The kerosene lamp was still in the middle of the table and two of the burners on the stove were left on. She opened the door to the utility room. Her mother had a laundry basket by the washing machine and she dropped her clothes in it. If the electricity didn't come back on soon, they'd never get caught up on the laundry.

She came back into the kitchen and went to the sink to get a drink of water. It would be a relief to go to bed, bringing the long day to a close. The events of the day had taken their toll on her. As she sat the glass down and turned to the door, she almost screamed.

There, leaning against the doorjamb, stood Ryan.

NINE

She backed away, ignoring the hurt in his eyes at her rejection of him.

"What do you want?"

"I came in for a drink of water." He paused, studying her. "What I want is another matter."

"Ryan—" she began to protest when he held up both hands.

"No, you don't have anything to worry about," he assured her bitterly. "I have no intention of attacking you."

His words brought the blood to her cheeks, not because she was embarrassed but because she felt guilty. He was not the only one responsible for what had happened earlier in the day. "It wasn't—all your fault."

"Thank you for that, at least." He took a step toward her and then stopped when she backed farther away. "Lisa, we have to talk about what happened."

She shook her head vehemently.

"I didn't use any protection."

She should've known better than to hope Ryan wouldn't think of all the implications. "I'm sure nothing happened. Don't worry about it."

This time he didn't stop. He reached out and seized her by the arms. "How can you say that? It's impossible to know this soon."

"I don't want to talk about it!" She was too confused right now.

"You can't just ignore—"

"Yes, I can!" she exclaimed fiercely. "Right now, I can. When—when I know—then I'll deal with it."

"But not alone," he said just as fiercely. "Do you understand me? Not alone."

"I understand," she whispered, keeping her head down. "Please, let me go to bed. I'm so tired."

He dropped his hands and Lisa brushed past him. She longed to bury her face in his chest, to feel his arms come around her and hold her, as he did in the attic. But she was also honest enough to admit that *she* wouldn't want it to end only in comfort. Until she figured out what she should do, her best course was to avoid Ryan, which wouldn't be easy since they were trapped in the same house.

She crossed the den to the fire and warmed her hands at the open flame. Her chills had less to do with the cold than they did with her attraction to Ryan. The kerosene lamp had been extinguished, and she stood there in the shadows of the fire, trying to focus on her problems.

The door to the den opened and she jumped as if she'd been shot.

"Did I scare you?" Paul whispered.

"Sorry. I was thinking."

"Where's Ryan? It's his turn upstairs."

"I believe he's in the kitchen." As soon as the door closed behind Paul, Lisa scrambled for the couch she was to share with her mother and Erin. She quietly lifted the covers and slid under them, trying not to disturb the others.

"Are you okay?" Erin whispered in the darkness.

"Yes. Sorry if I woke you."

''No, you didn't. I just—you seemed kind of distracted this evening.''

She mustn't have hidden her feelings as well as she'd hoped, Lisa realized. ''I'm fine.''

''I didn't say anything to upset you, did I?''

''No,'' Lisa whispered back.

''I mean, there have always been a lot of women chasing after Ryan. That doesn't mean he chases them back.''

''No, I know.'' In the short time they were married, Ryan hadn't had time for his wife, much less other women. She wasn't sure why Erin was trying to reassure her, however. Hopefully, it meant she didn't have to have Erin on her conscience for what had happened earlier in the day. She just had to worry about saving herself from the pain her actions could cause her.

A gentle snore from Margaret, sleeping in between them, brought a giggle from Erin. ''I should've worried about Margaret snoring, not Paul. Where are the guys, anyway?''

''Paul just came down from the bath, and I think it's Ryan's turn now. Aren't you sleepy?'' Lisa asked desperately. She didn't want to be awake when Ryan came back into the room.

''No, not really. I just—''

''What's all this talking in here?'' Paul whispered as he opened the door. ''You're supposed to be asleep.''

''I'm waiting for my bedtime story,'' Erin teased.

He moved over to their bed. ''You're in luck. I tell great bedtime stories to my niece. Of course, she always sits in my lap.''

''Mmm, maybe I'd better pass on the bedtime story.''

''Too bad. How about you, Lisa? Want to hear my bedtime story?''

''Thanks, anyway, Paul. I think I'll just go on to sleep.'' She lied, of course. She didn't think she'd ever get to sleep.

"What story does your niece like best?" Erin asked, sliding to a sitting position against the back of the couch.

"Cinderella is her favorite. Of course, she always thinks I'm Prince Charming," Paul said, walking over to the fire. Even without enough light to see his face, Lisa could hear the teasing in his voice.

"Just how old is your niece?" Erin demanded.

"Three."

Erin said nothing for a moment. Then she whispered, "Well, I think she has great taste." She slid back down under the covers and turned her back to Paul as he stood by the fireplace.

Lisa could see the outline of his body and watched as he started to move to the other side of their bed. She thought he wanted to ask Erin if she believed he could be *her* Prince Charming. The attraction the two felt was growing obvious. Lisa wished she could tell him to be grateful he couldn't.

Cinderella was a fairy tale. Real life didn't work out quite so easily. Paul would have the same difficulty with Erin that Lisa had with Ryan's background. She couldn't imagine Erin's family being happy for her to marry a schoolteacher.

The door opened again and Ryan entered.

"That was a fast shower," Paul commented softly.

"Yeah. All that was left was cold water."

"Sorry. I kept mine short."

"No problem. Are the others asleep?"

"Margaret is. The other two were awake a minute ago."

Lisa heard his footsteps and held very still. He rounded the bed and stood staring down at her. Then he squatted down beside her.

"Good night, Lisa," he whispered. Without warning, he leaned over and kissed her brow. He stood and turned to the fireplace, reaching for another log, before Lisa could react. Not that she intended to say or do anything.

Neither Erin nor Paul said anything about Ryan's behavior, but Lisa knew they must be wondering what was going on. She was kind of curious about that, too.

In the kitchen, he'd sounded angry with her. But his behavior now would indicate he still cared about her, as she did for him. But that didn't mean they could return to what they'd had. That was a fantasy, a dream world that had dissolved once reality touched it.

She watched as he laid another log on the fire and then replaced the screen. He sat down on the brick seat beside the fireplace.

"Not sleepy?" Paul asked as he settled down in the bed for the two of them.

"Not just yet. I thought I'd sit up for a while."

Lisa lay there in the darkness, staring at the dark form sitting by the fire. She'd never be able to go to sleep with him watching over her. She remembered once when she'd been very sick, her father had come to her bedroom and sat by her bed way into the night.

It had been such a comfort to see him beside her, taking care of her. Ryan's presence didn't comfort her, but he was still reaching out to her, as her father had. Her gaze drifted to the Christmas tree, its ornaments reflecting the firelight.

She'd lost her father and Ryan the same year. Now she'd lost the star. Would her life ever be normal again? Her father would tell her to do what's right and things would work out. Only she didn't know what was right. She only knew she ached for the happiness she'd found for just such a short time. She ached for her beloved father. And she ached for the man now sitting beside her bed.

Ryan knew she was still awake. Not that it mattered. He couldn't talk to her, touch her, here surrounded by the others. Not that she seemed willing to talk to him anyway. Her attitude ever since he arrived was to keep him at a distance.

Maybe he was crazy to think there was any hope of her listening to him. But he couldn't give up.

He looked at the Christmas tree. The holiday had a lot of meaning for Lisa. Her parents had celebrated it in special ways. Unlike his mother. His father had died five years ago. Ryan had taken over the company at the tender age of twenty-four, fresh out of college, with an MBA tucked under his arm.

By the time his father died, his parents' marriage had disintegrated to the point that they barely spoke to each other. Sharing the same house, they went their separate ways, meeting only for Ryan's sake.

At Christmastime, they'd each bought him presents and he opened them at different times, never together. His mother was always attending parties. He remembered one year when she'd gone on another cruise, leaving him with his father. The two of them had shared Christmas. Though they ate peanut butter sandwiches Christmas day, it was the best Christmas he'd had.

He wanted Lisa's kind of Christmas for his kids. He wanted Lisa's idea of marriage for himself. At least the kind of marriage her mother and father had shared. Maybe it was that warmth that had reached out to him when he first met her. He wasn't going to give up. The Christmas present he wanted this year was Lisa and all the warmth and love that came along with her.

He'd made a mistake, of course, planning a ski trip with Erin and her family. He and her family were old friends, but he couldn't abandon their daughter in the Texas Panhandle. He'd have to see she got to Colorado. Then he'd come back.

When he'd thought to stop here and talk to Frank, he wasn't sure what he wanted. He only knew he needed to see Lisa, talk to her. Once he'd done that, he knew what he'd wanted all along was Lisa.

With a sigh, he leaned back against the brick. Whatever it took, he'd do it. He stared at the mound of bed covers that hid her from him. She was his, whether she admitted it or not. And if she was carrying his child . . . The thought brought a smile to his face. He couldn't help it. Whatever the circumstances, Lisa's carrying his child made him happy.

The thought of Lisa in his arms, as she'd been that afternoon, brought other feelings to him. He wished he could crawl under the covers beside her and pull her into his arms. He'd be willing to stay put until spring arrived if he had her beside him.

Lisa stirred under the heavy covers, stretching out from the tight ball she'd slept in. Even though she hadn't opened her eyes, she suddenly knew she wasn't alone. When she looked, she discovered Ryan sitting in the opposite bed, leaning against the back of the sofa, staring at her.

"Where is everyone?"

"In the kitchen."

"Why are you in here?"

"I wasn't in any hurry."

She felt vulnerable, knowing he had watched her sleep. It suddenly brought to mind another time she'd awakened and found him watching her. Then she'd been pleased with his attention. But then they'd shared the bed—and much more.

Throwing back the covers, she sat up.

"Need any help?"

"No! No. I'm going upstairs to the bathroom."

She rushed out of the room without giving him the opportunity to stop her. When she reached the bathroom and looked in the mirror, she groaned. Her hair was a mess, and her face was pale from lack of sleep.

The mantel clock had struck two last night before she ever fell asleep. Ryan had still occupied his seat by the fireplace, so it was no wonder he, too, had been one of the last to awaken. She'd wanted to know what he was thinking, but she'd kept silent.

When she reached the bottom of the stairs a few minutes later, dressed in jeans and a sweater, green this time, and with her auburn hair pulled back with a matching scarf, she felt more in control of herself.

She bypassed the den and headed for the kitchen. Ryan was there ahead of her.

"Oh, good, we were just going to call you for breakfast," Erin said. She was wearing one of Margaret's aprons and carrying a platter of scrambled eggs.

"Sorry if I kept everyone waiting."

There were mumbles of acknowledgment from her mother and Paul, and Ryan smiled at her. She took her customary place between her mother and Paul, wondering if everyone else went short of sleep also.

Margaret brought her a cup of coffee and everyone sat down at the table. After a brief prayer, the plates of eggs, bacon, sausage, and toast were passed around the table.

"Now that everyone's here, I can tell you my good news," Margaret said.

"What's that, Mom?"

"I heard the early weather report on the radio. The storm is supposed to end some time today."

"What?" Erin exclaimed. "Oh."

Lisa stared at her. "Aren't you happy about it?"

"Yes, of course," she hurriedly said. "Of course I am. I was just surprised, that's all."

Lisa watched Ryan out of the corner of her eye. He had given no reaction to her mother's news. She looked at Paul, but he didn't appear any happier. What was wrong with everyone this morning?

"Well, since we've all been together these past few days, I thought it would be nice if we had our Christmas dinner tomorrow. It's Christmas Eve, and I doubt the roads will be open before noon."

Various protests were offered about the work it would

cause her, but Margaret rejected them all. "I'm going to cook a big Christmas dinner anyway. It'd be nice to have a full table to appreciate it." She paused before adding, "Besides, you've all made this a special Christmas. It'll be my way of saying thank you."

No one could refuse her plan after that. But conversation was lacking at the breakfast table. Paul asked Erin and Ryan about resuming their ski trip, and Erin left it up to Ryan to answer.

"Yeah, we'll meet her family there. At least we'll be able to join them for Christmas day."

"Are you going home for Christmas?" Erin asked Paul.

"I'll be leaving in a day or two. There's no rush. I have a big family. They won't miss me if I'm a couple of days late."

Lisa realized that in only a little over twenty-four hours, she'd be free of Ryan. A mixture of relief and melancholy filled her. As much as she was trying to avoid conversation with him, she loved being able to see him every day.

Once the meal was over, Margaret asked the men to fold up the sofas before they went to the barn to tend the animals.

"Do you want us to fold them up with the sheets still on them?" Paul asked.

"Yes, 'cause we'll use them again tonight. Lisa, why don't you and Erin go fold the quilts and pile them in a corner out of the way, along with the pillows? Then we can use the den in comfort until bedtime again."

"Yes, Mom."

The foursome trooped into the other room, and Lisa took one couch and Erin the other, each folding the linen.

"I guess we should bring in more wood," Ryan suggested to Paul. "They should be finished by the time we do that."

Paul nodded and followed Ryan out. Erin stared after them.

"Do you think something is bothering Paul?" she asked Lisa.

"I hadn't noticed. Maybe he's a little quieter than usual, but he probably didn't get a lot of sleep last night. These mattresses leave a lot to be desired."

"I suppose that could be it, but he hasn't teased me once this morning. I thought maybe I'd done something to offend him."

"I can't imagine what it would be. You didn't even beat him in Monopoly." Lisa smiled at the other's forlorn face.

"That wouldn't bother Paul. He's not macho at all."

"Don't let him hear you say that, or he *would* be offended."

"I meant it in a good way. Neither he nor Ryan has to beat up other people to prove he's strong. That's what I meant." She carried her folded quilts over to the corner. "I hate those kind of men."

"Me, too. But you're right. Paul isn't like that."

"Neither is Ryan."

"No, neither is Ryan."

The two men came in with arm loads of wood.

"Finished?" Ryan asked, coming to stand beside Lisa.

She tried to casually walk away toward the door to the kitchen, but she was afraid Ryan was offended. "Yes, all finished."

Folding up the sofas took only seconds. Erin helped put the sofa cushions back in place, then all three joined Lisa at the door to return to the kitchen.

"All done in there, Mom. I'll take over the dish washing now."

"Oh, good. I want to get started baking. Boys, will you take care of the animals now?" Margaret was in her element, organizing and baking, her two favorite things to do.

"Right away, Margaret. And I'll be careful with the eggs," Ryan added, smiling, before she could say anything.

"I know you will. You're both so helpful. Bundle up well." She resumed the search in her cookbook for a favorite recipe and never noticed Paul rolling his eyes at Lisa.

"She forgets you're grown men," Lisa whispered to him.

"I do, too, when she talks to me like that."

His grumble didn't have the lightness he usually put into such remarks, and she looked at him more closely. Something was certainly bothering him, as Erin had thought. She wondered what it was.

She followed the men into the utility room as they shrugged on their coats and took down the knit scarves and hats hanging on a hook.

"Paul, are you all right?"

He gave her a hard look, not bothering to smile. "I'm fine."

Her question caught Ryan's attention. "Paul, if you don't feel well, I'm sure I could manage to milk Betsy this morning. Why don't you stay here where it's warm?"

"I said I'm fine. I don't need you doing my chores for me!" he snarled before wrapping the scarf around his face and opening the door. Without waiting for Ryan, he disappeared into the swirling snow, pulling the door closed behind him.

"He certainly got up on the wrong side of the bed this morning," Ryan commented. "Do you think he's coming down with something?"

"I hope not. Maybe he's worried about something."

"Well, I'll see if I can find out while we're out in the barn. Some men don't like to talk about their problems in front of women." He pulled off his glove and ran a finger down the side of Lisa'a face and then held her chin while his lips brushed gently across hers. "I'll be back as soon as I can."

"Don't hurry on my account," Lisa grumbled, backing

away from him. "Besides, you're not exploring the North Pole. You're just going out to the barn."

"When I'm away from you, it feels like it's halfway around the world, sweetheart."

With that remark, he left, leaving Lisa standing in the utility room with her mouth open.

TEN

Ryan fought his way to the barn, wondering if Margaret's weather prediction could possibly be right. Surely the storm would've lessened some if it was drawing to an end.

He reached the barn and slipped into its relative warmth with relief. In its shadowy twilight, he didn't see Paul. Looking around, he found him leaning against the wall near the door, as if waiting for him.

"Is everything all right?" he asked.

"No. It's not. I finally figured out something last night."

Ryan frowned. "What did you figure out?"

"You're Lisa's ex-husband, aren't you?"

"Is that what's put you in such a bad mood?" he asked curiously.

"Yeah. Because I think you've been harassing Lisa since you've been here, and I was too busy to notice."

"What Lisa and I do has nothing to do with you."

Paul stepped toward him, his hands clenched. "Wrong. Lisa is my friend. She suffered a lot because of her marriage to you. I don't think she should have to suffer anymore."

"What are you talking about?" Ryan demanded. "Do you think I walked out on her? Is that what she told you?"

"She didn't tell me anything. I can't get her to talk about it. I just know you hurt her badly."

"Listen, Paul—"

"No, you listen to me. Just leave her alone." He turned and stomped away, but not before Ryan caught him by the arm.

"You don't need to tell me what to do about Lisa. That's between the two of us. I'm not trying to hurt her. But I do want to work things out. I want her back," he said firmly, wanting Paul to understand he was staking his claim.

"What if she doesn't want to come back?"

"She does." Ryan's chin came up. He wouldn't let anyone convince him differently either. Except Lisa.

"I don't think so." Paul glowered at him, his features tense.

"I don't care what you think. This is between Lisa and me. You stay out of it."

"She needs *someone* to protect her, and her father's gone," Paul insisted.

"You're being ridiculous, Paul. Lisa doesn't need you to protect her from me." Paul said nothing, only frowning at him. Clearly, Ryan wouldn't be able to convince the man.

"Come on. Let's get on with the chores so we can get back to the house."

"Fine. I'll take care of Betsy. You do your thing with the chickens." Paul turned his back on him and reached for the stool. Ryan turned away only to spin around when Paul called "Betsy?" in a panicky voice.

"What is it?" He stared at Paul, trying to discern any problems in the shadowy barn.

"Where is Betsy?" Paul demanded, as if Ryan had stolen her.

Ryan ran to Paul's side and they hurried to the spot

Betsy usually occupied. They found the cow lying on her side.

"Is she dead?" Paul asked in horror.

Ryan laid his hand on her large stomach. "No, she's breathing, but I don't know anything about cows."

"Don't look at me. I'm certainly no expert."

The two men stared at each other, their earlier anger forgotten.

"What do we do?"

"One of us will have to go back to the house and tell Margaret," Ryan said firmly. "Hopefully, she'll know what to do."

Just as Ryan was about to volunteer to carry the urgent message, they heard someone trying to get in the barn door.

"It's not fair," Erin complained. She was sitting at the kitchen table breaking pecan halves into smaller pieces while Lisa cut up boiled eggs for the pea salad her mother had planned.

"What's not fair? Being snowed in?" Lisa asked with a smile.

"No. I mean, that's not fair, but I've enjoyed myself. It's not fair that the guys get to go to the barn every morning."

Lisa raised her eyebrows in surprise. "I think they might agree with you that it's not fair that they have to go to the barn. But we can't abandon the animals."

"No, you don't understand. I don't think it's fair that I *don't* get to go to the barn," Erin explained, giving Lisa a wry smile.

"You *want* to go to the barn?" Lisa cast a swift look at the window. Outside the storm still blew white and opaque.

"Well, at least it would be a change of scenery, some excitement."

Lisa weighed Erin's request. She'd vowed not to return

to the barn with Ryan, but if Erin and Paul were there, there really wasn't any reason not to. And if it made the morning more exciting for Erin, she supposed it was worth it.

"Okay. I'll take you to the barn."

"You will?" Erin jumped from her chair. "I'll go get my coat." She stopped when she saw Margaret watching her. "Oh, Margaret, I forgot about the pecans. Do you need them right away?"

"No, Erin. You go with Lisa. Just be sure to hold on to that rope." Margaret's indulgent smile reassured her, and Erin raced from the kitchen. After she'd disappeared, Margaret shook her head and muttered, "Crazy."

"Not really, Mom. We'll finish these things when we get back. By the time we get out there, the guys should be finished with the chores, so it won't take long."

Erin ran back into the room, shrugging into her coat. "This is exciting. I've never been outside in a blizzard."

"And I hope you never are again. A blizzard is dangerous," Lisa reminded her. "Whatever you do, don't turn loose of the rope, okay?"

"Of course not. And I brought a scarf down so I could tie it behind my head just like you do." She held up her scarf to show she was prepared.

"Come on, my coat's in the utility room."

In a matter of minutes, the two young women were ready.

"I'll go first. Put your right hand on my shoulder and your left on the rope. Ready?"

"Ready."

Lisa opened the door and Erin felt the force of the wind for the first time. Even over the roar of the storm Lisa heard her gasp. She grinned beneath her scarf. Erin was going to get her money's worth.

The snow was deeper than the last time Lisa had made the trek. There was no sign of the men's footprints in the two feet of snow. The wind had already obliterated them.

Lisa trudged forward, her head down. Erin's hand on her shoulder assured her she hadn't lost her partner.

When they finally reached the barn, Lisa fumbled with the latch for the door. She was stiff from the cold.

Finally, she got it opened and pulled herself and Erin through the door. They shoved the door shut together and then stamped their feet and brushed off their coats before they looked around.

"Paul?" Lisa called.

"Thank God. Lisa, come here."

All she could think of was an accident to Ryan. Her heart thumping, fear drying her mouth, she raced across the dark barn. "What's wrong?"

"It's Betsy," Ryan's voice called out.

Lisa's tension eased slightly as she recognized Ryan's voice before his words made sense. "Betsy? What's wrong with her?" She reached them to discover the cow down on the barn floor. "Is she dead?" she asked, fear in her voice. Betsy was like a member of the family.

"She's breathing," Ryan assured her, taking her arm, "but we don't know what's wrong with her. Do you?"

Lisa knelt by the cow's head. "Betsy, poor old girl, what's the matter?"

The cow moaned, but Lisa had no idea what was wrong. She stood up. "I'll have to go get Mom."

"I'll go," Ryan immediately offered. "You stay with Betsy. At least you're familiar to her."

Lisa touched his hand in gratitude. "Thanks. Try—try not to worry her too much."

"Right." He tied the knit scarf around his face and hurried out into the storm.

"Is she going to be all right?" Erin asked, her voice tentative.

"What are you doing out here?" Paul snapped, spinning around.

"Well, don't bother putting out the welcome mat," Erin snapped back. "I just wanted to get out of the house."

"That's a fool thing to do. No one should come out here unless they have to. That's a blizzard out there!"

"No fake, Jake!" Erin shouted in return.

Betsy moaned again and Lisa said, "Please, if you're going to argue, go over by the chickens and do it quietly. You're upsetting Betsy."

"Sorry," Paul muttered, turning his back on both women.

Erin walked to his side and whispered, "What's wrong with you, Paul? Did I do something to make you angry?"

Lisa, too, was curious. Unflappable Paul, with a sense of humor always ready, had lost his cool over a minor thing. She didn't think it could all be attributed to worry over Betsy.

"Of course not," he responded to Erin's question. "I'm just concerned about—about whatever-her-name-is."

There was no warmth in his voice, only impatience and a touch of pain. Lisa wondered what could be upsetting him. She stroked Betsy's flat forehead and waited.

Nothing else was said. Before the strain could get too bad, Margaret and Ryan arrived in the barn. Margaret hurried over to her cow. "How is she?" she asked Lisa.

"I don't know, Mom. She just moans every once in a while and doesn't show any inclination to move."

Margaret moved back from the cow, staring down at her, a frown on her face. She leaned down and put her hand flat against the cow's belly. "Hmmm."

"What is it?" Lisa asked.

"I'm not sure," Margaret muttered, but she'd turned her attention to the rest of the barn instead of the cow. "Ryan," she called.

"Yes, Margaret?"

"Have you fed the chickens yet? Have you gotten out the feed?"

"No. Before I got over to the bin, Paul called that something was wrong with Betsy."

Margaret walked across the small barn to the door of

the storage room where the chicken feed was stored. It was standing open. "I think I've found the problem, unless you've fed the chickens five or six buckets of feed."

"No, only one the past two days."

"I think you didn't completely latch the door and Betsy stuffed herself with chicken feed." Margaret turned to walk back to her cow's side.

"Damn, I'm sorry, Margaret," Ryan said, horrified at the problem he'd caused. "What can we do?"

"She won't die, will she?" Erin asked.

"No, she won't die. She'll just have a stomachache for a couple of days. She won't give much milk, and what she does won't be fit for consumption, but I've got more than enough milk as it is."

Ryan tried to apologize again, but Margaret waved it aside. "Don't browbeat yourself about it. She'll recover. I've seen Lisa in the same situation, only it was caused by cotton candy. It's painful, but maybe she'll learn a lesson." Margaret laughed. "Lisa certainly did. To this day, she won't touch cotton candy."

"Mom! You don't have to tell all my nasty little secrets, do you?" Lisa complained, though with a smile, relieved to find that Betsy would recover.

"Confession is good for the soul, dear," Margaret said, before snapping her fingers. "Oops, I left something on the stove. I've got to get back to the house."

"But what do we do for Betsy?" Ryan asked.

"Nothing. I'll come back later in the day and check on her." As she was going out the door, she called, "Don't forget to feed the chickens and bring in the eggs." Then the door shut behind her and the barn was still once more.

From the shadows where she'd retreated, Erin asked, "Can I collect the eggs? I've never done that before."

"Sure," Ryan said. "That's my job, and if I can do it, I know you can." He went to the storage room and brought out the feed for the chickens before carefully latching the door. "I don't want to make the same mistake twice."

He fed the chickens and then directed Erin to collect the eggs. While she was doing so, he moved over next to Lisa. "I didn't think to ask what you two are doing out here. Did you think we needed help?"

"No, Erin was anxious to get out of the house."

Paul shoved his way between the two of them. "Ready to go back to the house, Lisa? There's no need to wait for them."

Lisa stared at her friend. What was wrong with him this morning?

"I told you, Paul—" Ryan began.

"And I told you. Come on, Lisa." Paul grabbed her by the arm and pulled her toward the door.

"Paul, what are you doing?" she demanded, digging in her heels.

"I'll explain when we get to the house," he muttered.

Lisa looked back at Ryan. He nodded, as if to say everything was all right. She half waved her hand before she had to brace herself for the storm.

"Are you all right?" Ryan asked Erin as she stood silently beside the chicken roosts.

"Yes, I guess so."

"Did you get all the eggs?"

"I found seven."

"That sounds about right. Come on, let's go back to the house." He was anxious to see if Lisa accepted Paul's protection.

"Ryan, what was that all about? Did you and Paul have an argument?"

"Sort of," he said, wrapping his scarf around his face.

"Wait. Explain to me what's going on."

She'd planted herself between him and the door, her hands on her hips, waiting for an explanation.

With a sigh, he pushed down his scarf. "Paul just figured out my connection to Lisa."

"But—but why is he so angry?"

"He thinks I hurt Lisa before and might hurt her now. He says he's her friend and he's going to protect her from me."

"Then—he must love her," Erin said slowly.

Ryan couldn't see her eyes, but he heard the pain in her voice. "Don't tell me you've fallen in love with him," he protested. "Come on, Erin, you've known him only two days."

"How long did it take you to fall in love with Lisa?"

He gave a half grin and patted her on the shoulder. "Okay, point taken."

He and Erin had grown up as neighbors in Dallas. He'd treated her as his little sister all these years, in spite of his mother's fondest dreams that they would marry.

Wrapping his arm around her shoulder, he said, "I don't think he's in love with Lisa. Anyway, I don't think she's in love with him. And I intend to make sure of it."

"Are you offering me the leftovers?"she said with a sniff.

"Nope. I'm just telling you they'll be there. What you do with him is up to you." He moved them toward the door. "It serves you right, you know."

"What does?"

"Falling in love with him. You wouldn't have met him if you hadn't tried to meddle in my business."

"Ryan Hall! You know I only had your best interests at heart. Your mother told me Lisa was terrible, that she was only after your money and would sink her clutches in you as soon as you turned up on her doorstep." Erin had come to a halt and turned to face him again.

"And you know better than to believe my mother."

"I know," she agreed with a sigh. "It's just that you've been so unhappy, I was afraid—I just want you to be happy."

"And now that you've met Lisa?" He waited for her opinion. They were good friends. He wanted her to like Lisa.

"She's terrific. And I hope you do remarry. I think she'll make you very happy."

Ryan gave her a hug. "Thanks, honey. I know she'll make me happy. I have to worry about making her happy."

"Well, I'm rooting for you."

"Thanks. Let's get back to where there's a little warmth. I won't stand a chance if I leave Sir Galahad alone with her for very long."

Lisa shoved the door closed, shutting out the storm. Yanking down her scarf, she turned to the man accompanying her. "What was that all about?"

Instead of answering her question, he asked one of his own. "Why didn't you tell me he was your ex-husband?"

"Ryan told you?"

"No. I figured it out on my own from some of the things that were said. Why didn't you tell me?"

She turned her back to him as she shrugged out of her coat. His question wasn't easy to answer. Finally, she said, "I thought at first they'd be here only a few hours. It didn't seem necessary to tell you." She faced him again and shrugged. "After I realized the storm was going to go on for several days . . . I don't know. It just seemed easier to not say anything."

Paul stepped closer and took her shoulders in his hands. "I could've protected you if you'd told me."

"Paul, we're not out on a battlefield. This is my home," Lisa protested. "I don't need protection here."

"You're telling me he hasn't tried anything? Hasn't hurt you?" Paul stared at her, searching for an answer.

Lisa pulled herself from his grasp. She couldn't face him and lie. Finally, she said, "You can't protect me from myself, Paul. That's the difficulty. Yes, Ryan has—has tried to—''

"What? What's he done to you?''

Lisa closed her eyes. "Paul,'' she whispered in desperation, "don't you see? I'm as much of the problem as Ryan is.''

"Lisa? Is that you?'' Margaret called from the kitchen. "Is everything all right?''

"Everything's fine, Mom,'' she called and backed toward the kitchen door. "Paul, I'll talk to you later. I can't discuss this now.''

"I'll be here. And I'll do what I can to protect you.''

"Paul—''

"Lisa?'' Margaret called again.

Lisa shrugged her shoulders and entered the kitchen. She couldn't explain her relationship with Ryan to Paul. She didn't even understand it herself. More and more she was coming to realize that she shared the blame for their failed marriage. That didn't mean they could make a go of it. She still felt their different backgrounds made it impossible. Didn't she?

"Where are the others?'' Margaret asked.

"Ryan and Erin stayed to feed the chickens and gather the eggs.'' She took a deep breath, hoping her voice didn't show the strain the day was already providing.

"And Paul?'' Margaret asked just as the door opened and Paul stepped into the kitchen.

"I'm right here, Margaret, next to Lisa. And that's where I'm going to stay.'' His voice was as inflexible as his words.

Lisa didn't know if that was a threat or a promise.

ELEVEN

Noise from the utility room announced the arrival of Erin and Ryan. Lisa opened the door.

"Did you have any problems?" she asked.

"No, except we're half frozen," Ryan said with a grin.

"How about you, Erin? Did you like going to the barn?" Lisa watched as Erin brushed the snow from herself.

"Y-yes, but it was much worse than I thought it would be out there. The snow looks so pretty and soft from in here."

"That's the way life is," Paul said roughly, speaking over Lisa's shoulder. "Those who are sheltered don't realize just how difficult it is."

Erin's eyes widened and she stared at him. "Are you trying to say something about me?" she demanded.

Lisa almost groaned out loud. It was going to be a long day if Paul continued in this vein. "How about a cup of coffee to warm you up?" she asked, hoping to distract everyone.

"Sounds good to me," Ryan replied, nudging Erin. "How about you, Erin? Want some coffee?"

She continued to glare at Paul, ignoring the others.

Lisa turned around and pushed Paul back, muttering to him as she did so, "Don't start a fight."

"I wasn't," he protested. "I just made a general statement."

"Well, keep it to yourself." She had enough to worry about without Paul starting anything.

"Mom, I'm going to make coffee for everyone if I won't be in your way."

Margaret nodded but kept on with her work. "Why don't you put it on a tray and take it to the den? That way I won't disturb you."

Lisa translated that to mean her mother didn't want them all cluttering up the kitchen. "Okay. Why don't you all go into the den and warm by the fire? I'll bring the coffee in as soon as it's ready."

"I'll stay and help," Ryan immediately said.

"No! *I'll* stay and help," Paul said, shoving his way in front of Ryan as if they were in a race.

Lisa rolled her eyes. It was going to be a *very* long day. "Thank you both, but I can manage on my own. Just go in the den, and try not to come to blows before I bring the coffee."

There was a glimmer of laughter in Ryan's eyes that lightened Lisa's heart, but Paul continued to glower at everyone. Erin, standing forgotten, walked to the door. "Let me know if you need some *real* help, Lisa," she said before disappearing in the direction of the den.

At least someone was doing what she'd asked. Lisa pleaded with her eyes in a look at Ryan, and he nodded before following Erin, leaving only Paul.

"Listen, Paul, we've got twenty-four hours left, probably. Would you please try to keep everything calm until the storm is over?"

Suddenly looking weary, Paul shrugged his shoulders. "I'll try."

"Thanks. I'll bring the coffee in as soon as it's ready."

Lisa breathed a sigh of relief as the door closed behind

him. She turned to the stove to put on the water for the coffee.''

"Poor Paul," Margaret murmured.

"What, Mom? Why would you say that?"

"Because you shouldn't have invited him, dear. I think he must've thought the invitation meant more than it did.'' She continued to stir whatever she was mixing, not looking at her daughter.

Standing still, Lisa let out a long breath. "It did at the time, Mom. Only now, I realize—I realize I don't love him.''

"Well, no, dear. I'd hoped you might've gotten over Ryan, but it's obvious you haven't.''

"Mom! That's not true. I—''

"Don't waste your breath denying what I can see perfectly well with my own eyes." Margaret put down her spoon and turned to face Lisa. "Neither one of you can keep your eyes off each other.''

Her cheeks flaming, Lisa turned to take down four cups from the cabinet. She couldn't think of anything to say to her mother.

"So, what are you going to do about it?"

Lisa set the four cups down and pulled out a tray from the cabinet. "I don't know."

Margaret gave her daughter a hug and then turned her so they were facing. "Have you told him you still love him?''

"No!" Lisa exclaimed, panic in her heart. "No, Mom, I haven't done that. Whether or not I care about Ryan isn't the issue.''

"It's not? Things must've changed a lot since I was young," Margaret muttered.

"Mom, I loved him when I divorced him, but—but we had nothing in common. He didn't take the time to try to understand me. He just expected me to live the kind of life his mother lived. Period. We didn't talk about anything.''

"You said he was involved in some heavy-duty business things. Maybe he didn't have any time right then."

Lisa's eyes filled with tears and she blinked furiously, trying to keep them from falling. "I know he didn't. But his mother—he could've—I don't know, Mom. I'm so confused," she wailed.

"Your father always said to trust your heart, dear. It's much wiser than the head." She patted Lisa on the back. "Now, fix that coffee or those three will be back in here to find out what's going on, and I'll get nothing done."

Lisa wiped her eyes and got on with fixing the coffee. Hopefully she had learned a lot since she'd married Ryan, too. Perhaps that hard-earned wisdom would help as well. When the tray was ready, she paused to murmur, "Thanks, Mom, for listening."

"Of course. I love you, dear. And don't you forget that," Margaret said, giving a response she'd used for many years.

"No, I never will." With a smile, Lisa lifted the tray and headed for the den, where, unless a miracle had occurred, three rather unhappy people awaited her.

Ryan followed Erin into the den, feeling better than he had. At least Lisa had rejected Paul's offer as well as his own. He hoped that indicated she didn't feel a need for protection against him—at least not while they were surrounded by others. If Ryan tried to get her alone, she probably wouldn't budge. He couldn't really blame her.

In fact, it would be better for his plans if they weren't alone. They really did need to talk, but he found it difficult to pass up an opportunity to hold her in his arms. And once he did that, things rapidly escaped his control.

Paul came in and moved to the opposite end of the large den from where Erin was staring out the window. He paused to study some prints on the wall. Ryan couldn't help but feel that Paul was fighting his attraction to Erin. Whether it was because he felt guilty about Lisa or whether, like Lisa, he felt that Erin's wealth was a problem, he didn't know.

"It's not too cold in here, is it? It's hard to believe the fireplace could keep this room so warm with the storm outside," Ryan said, hoping conversation would draw the other two to a middle ground.

"Insulation," Paul said tersely, not turning around.

Erin said nothing, continuing to stare outside.

So much for his efforts at diplomacy. He searched for a topic of conversation that would draw them both in, but nothing came to mind. He wandered over to the fireplace, watching the logs pop and crackle as the flames consumed them.

"So, where does your family live?" Ryan finally asked Paul. He could think of nothing else.

"Cleburne."

"By Lake Whitney?" The large lake, southwest of Dallas by about an hour and a half, was a favorite of Ryan's when he had a chance to get away.

"Yes."

Ryan wondered if Paul intended to answer every question directed at him with one word the rest of the day. If so, their conversations would be limited.

Erin, however, turned around slowly and stared at Paul. "Your family is from Cleburne?"

"Yes," he repeated, frustration in his voice. "That's what I said."

"Well, excuse me for asking. I was just surprised," Erin whipped back, her eyes flashing anger.

Ryan sighed. Maybe one-word answers weren't so bad, after all.

"What's the matter? Did you think everyone came from Dallas? Or does that label me as a small-town hick?" Paul challenged, moving a few steps toward Erin.

"Why don't you take that chip off your shoulder," she replied, walking toward him. "I was surprised because my father is from Cleburne."

Paul seemed stunned by that pronouncement. "He is? So how did he make all his money? Certainly not in Cleburne."

"You've never heard of Steward Lumber?" she demanded, watching him.

"Yeah, I've heard of it. But he couldn't make millions off that."

"No one said he made millions," she returned.

Ryan felt as though he were watching a tennis match. However, he couldn't let Erin get away with that response. He cleared his throat and cocked an eyebrow at her.

"Well, maybe he does, but no one said so," she mumbled.

Paul gave a derisive laugh.

"What difference does it make to you, anyway?" she challenged. "You're acting like he's committed a sin just because he's been successful."

Lisa entered the room with the coffee tray in time to hear Erin's remark. She paused and looked at Ryan, a question in her eyes. He shrugged his shoulders. He wasn't sure himself what was going on, and he'd been in the room the entire time.

"Coffee's ready," Lisa announced, carrying the tray to the coffee table.

Erin and Paul didn't move, as if afraid to get that close to each other. Lisa looked at them expectantly and then looked to Ryan.

"Come on, Erin. The coffee's going to get cold." He moved over to Lisa's side and deliberately placed a hand on her shoulder. As if Ryan had blown a whistle, Paul rushed over to Lisa. With a wink at her, Ryan moved over to the other couch, leaving the place beside Lisa vacant for Paul.

Erin joined Ryan on his sofa and thanked Lisa for the cup of coffee she offered her. "I see you brought Christmas cookies for our snack. I need to get that recipe from your mom. They have a unique flavor."

Paul snorted, setting down his coffee cup.

"You didn't care for the cookies?" Erin asked offended, as if they were talking about her own prized recipe.

"The cookies were delicious," he replied, reaching for one as if to underline his response.

"Then why did you laugh?"

Ryan leaned back on the sofa, beginning to see the humor in the exchanges. If these two kept up this kind of conversation all day, they wouldn't have to search for entertainment. His gaze sought Lisa and he winked at her again. Her faint smile made him want to smooth away the frown on her forehead. And touch her cheeks. And kiss—there he went again. He'd better concentrate on the conversation.

"Because I can't see you baking anything." The scorn in his voice drew a look of surprise from Lisa, but Erin rose to the taunt like a bull to a red flag.

"I am perfectly capable of baking cookies!"

"I don't doubt it. But rich people just have them delivered, dear heart. They don't actually soil their hands baking them themselves." Paul looked down his nose in a superior fashion.

"I think you've watched too much *Dynasty*," Erin protested. "We have a housekeeper, but Mother frequently cooks dinner, and she always bakes our birthday cakes."

"Mrs. Hall never entered the kitchen," Lisa said quietly. "Maybe your family is different, Erin, but she didn't bother with—with things like that."

Ryan studied his ex-wife. He'd already begun to wonder if the time Lisa spent with his mother wasn't part of the problem. Now he cleared his throat again. "My mother is difficult about a lot of things, Lisa. But I'm not sure the money is the cause of it. I don't think she would've been interested in making a home wherever she lived."

Lisa seemed stunned by his words. Erin hurried to support him. "He's right, Lisa. Mrs. Hall isn't—isn't the homebody type."

"And your mother is?" Paul sneered. "I can just see her in a designer apron whipping up breakfast."

"And I think you're a snob in reverse!" Erin exclaimed, jumping up from the sofa and returning to her position by the window across the room. However, everyone saw the tears in her eyes before she walked away.

Lisa stared at her before turning to Paul. "Don't you think you were a little hard on her?"

"The truth hurts," he muttered.

"But that's not the truth about Erin's family," Ryan said quietly. "I won't deny that there are wealthy families who are ostentatious, rude, demanding and have all the other stereotypes apply to them. But there are stereotypes about teachers, too. I doubt that you subscribe to those."

Paul's cheeks flushed and he looked guilty. "No. No, I don't. Maybe I was a little harsh, but—"

"A little?" Lisa prodded gently. "Erin hasn't acted the least bit like a prima donna since they arrived. She's done her share of the work without any complaint and been cheerful in a difficult situation."

"Yeah." Paul studied his cup of coffee.

"I think now would be a good time to go apologize," Lisa added.

With a gusty sigh, he set his coffee cup on the table and stood up. Shoving his hands in his pockets, he ambled over to the window, trying to look nonchalant.

"Do you think that will stop the war?" Ryan asked, smiling at Lisa. He debated moving over to Paul's seat, but he thought he'd be better off staying out of reach.

"It can't hurt. I don't understand what's come over Paul. He's usually so agreeable." She kept her eyes on the other couple, avoiding Ryan's gaze.

"Was my mother difficult to live with?" he asked abruptly, watching as her eyes widened and she turned to him, surprised.

"What? Why would you ask such a thing?"

"Because the two of you aren't much alike."

"No, we're not, but she was—was hospitable."

He watched her hands twist in her lap and knew she wasn't telling him the whole story. "Did you ever ask yourself why I married you?"

The color in her cheeks flamed and he longed to run his fingers down them.

"We've already discussed that," she muttered, looking away.

"Besides that, sweetheart," he teased, glad the thought of their lovemaking didn't leave her unmoved. It certainly affected him. Even thinking about it brought the inevitable reaction. He sat up and leaned forward.

Before she could answer, Erin and Paul, forgotten by Ryan, returned to the coffee table. He saw the relief in Lisa's eyes that she wasn't forced to continue their private discussion.

He leaned back, resigned. Resolving their difficulties would have to wait for privacy. But he had no intention of giving up. After the holidays, when Lisa returned to town, he would court her nonstop. They could learn to be friends before he again became her lover. He sighed. He hoped his patience would last.

"I'm sorry for my behavior," Erin said to Lisa. "I—I sometimes have a quick temper."

"I think it was justified this time. Men can be so difficult," she added, slanting a look at Ryan.

"But how can you live without us?" he asked, tempting her with a smile.

Lisa's chin came up and she looked down her nose at him. "Very well, thank you."

He stared at her, tracing her features with his gaze, wanting to take her into his arms. Finally, as she blushed again, he murmured, "You may be able to manage without me, sweetheart, but I can't manage without you."

His words shook her, he realized, as she set her cup

down on the table to keep it from rattling in her shaking hands. Good. He wanted her to realize he was serious in his pursuit of her.

Erin looked at Lisa and came up with a different topic of conversation. "Did you know Paul and my father are from the same town?"

Lisa smiled at her gratefully. "Oh, really? What town is that?"

"Cleburne."

"Did they know each other?" Lisa asked. Ryan felt she was reaching a little for a conversational topic.

When Erin started to demur, Paul said, "Actually, my father knew—knows Erin's father."

"You never said that!" Erin exclaimed.

"I didn't realize it until you mentioned Steward Lumber," he said defensively. "Besides, it was a long time ago. They grew up together."

"What's your father's name? Dad will want to know," Erin said, smiling.

"Richard Bellows. But your father probably won't remember. After all, it was a long time ago."

"Your father remembers. Why wouldn't Dad?" Erin reasoned.

"Because your father is the local success story. Everyone always remembers that person." Paul studied the coffee in his mug, avoiding Erin's look.

"I think he'll remember. I'll let you know when we get home from snow skiing."

"Yeah. Sure." In those two words, Paul managed to convey his skepticism quite clearly to everyone.

Since that conversational gambit seemed dead, Ryan searched for another, but nothing came to mind. It seemed Erin was equally interested in finding some way to occupy their morning.

"Does anyone want to play more Monopoly?" she suggested.

"No," Lisa groaned. "It takes too long."

"How about cards?" Ryan suggested, trying to help.

The others mulled over that suggestion. Finally, Lisa asked, "What card games does everyone know?"

"Bridge?" Erin suggested.

Paul curled his lip at her suggestion but fortunately didn't voice his opinion.

"How about spades?" Lisa offered. "That takes less work than bridge, and I don't feel like concentrating."

"I don't know how to play spades," Erin said, frowning.

"If you play bridge, spades will be a cinch," Paul assured her. Ryan thought it was the first decent thing he'd said to Erin all morning.

"Why don't you explain the game to Erin while I find a deck of cards and paper to keep score?" Lisa said. "You play spades, don't you, Ryan?"

"Yes, but it's been a while. Will you take a chance on being my partner? It wouldn't be fair to put two novice players together," he reminded her, nodding toward Erin.

She glanced nervously at Paul before agreeing. "I suppose so. Is that all right with you, Paul, if you and Erin are partners and Ryan and I pair up?"

Paul looked up from his discussion with Erin. "Sure. In fact, if we play right here, we're already seated in the right places, opposite each other."

"Good. I'll just take the tray back to the kitchen and—" Lisa began.

"I'll take the tray to the kitchen. You take care of finding the cards," Ryan said. That would give the other two longer to explain the game. He picked up the tray after everyone set their cups on it and took it to the kitchen. After he talked to Margaret a minute, he came back to the hallway and waited, leaning against the wall.

"What are you doing?" Lisa asked in surprise, coming to an abrupt halt as she reached the last step.

"Waiting for you."

"Why?"

He saw the apprehension in her eyes. "Lisa, I'm not going to make love to you right here in the hallway. There's no need to be so worried."

She took the last step off the stairway. "Of course not. I wasn't worried."

"Like hell you weren't. I could see it in your eyes."

"Ryan, don't—"

"I think you've used those two words more than any in your vocabulary since I got here." He pushed away from the wall and took several steps closer to her, keeping his hands in his pockets.

She watched him, her eyes growing larger as he moved closer. "With good reason."

"It hasn't all been bad, has it?"

"No," she said slowly. "You've been very supportive sometimes, Ryan, and sweet to Mom."

"And to you, I hope," he suggested, moving one step closer.

She leaned back until he was afraid she'd tip over. "Y-yes, of course."

"So don't I deserve a reward?"

Her eyes were wary, but he noticed a growing twinkle in them, too. "More sugar cookies?"

He grinned. "No, I think I lost interest in cookies yesterday afternoon. I had something else in mind."

She didn't answer except by raising one brow.

He took one hand from his pocket and ran a finger down her cheek. "If I promise not to get carried away, how about one kiss?"

"I don't think that's a good idea."

"Why not?"

"It—it makes us—"

"Want more?" he suggested softly, watching her.

She raised her chin, as if determined not to be embarrassed. "Yes."

"Nothing could make me want you more than I already

do, sweetheart." He stood patiently, waiting for her to think about what he'd said.

She frowned and he reached up to smooth away the wrinkle on her forehead. Taking a step back, she shook her head. "We're supposed to be friends, Ryan. That's what you said."

"And I'm trying to be friendly," he assured her, narrowing the distance between them again. He took hold of her shoulders. "One kiss won't do any harm."

"Yes, it will. Only I can't figure out how to explain it," she complained, frustration on her face.

"Well, while you're thinking about it—" he began but stopped to take the kiss he wanted.

"Ryan—" she began, but his mouth stopped any further complaint.

TWELVE

The magic of Ryan's touch enveloped Lisa at once. Even so, she knew she'd been right.

No matter what logic he used, when he touched her, she was in trouble. He'd made sense until his lips touched hers. Now, if she could forget the past, they'd go right up the stairs to the bedroom. But she couldn't.

She opened her mouth to his, responding to his pressure to deepen the kiss. Now she not only had to fight his urgings but also had to fight her own response.

When he lifted his lips from hers, he muttered, out of breath, "See? That didn't hurt anything."

Swallowing, she whispered, "Then why do we both sound like we just ran a marathon?"

"That's not the point."

"Oh?" she said, still held in his arms. "Just what is the point, then?"

"The point is, I didn't drag you up the stairs and make love to you like I want to."

Her heart beat double-time, just thinking about it, and she felt his body stir against her. "But you haven't turned me loose yet, either."

"There's another good point," he said with a wide grin

that brought an answering smile to her lips. The grin faded as he stared down at her. "It just feels so good to hold you, it's hard to let you go."

His words squeezed her heart. How many times since the divorce had she lain in bed alone, aching for his touch? Desperate for a distraction, she asked, "What about the others?"

"Let them find their own entertainment."

They probably could. In fact, she'd come to the conclusion she didn't have to worry about breaking Paul's heart. She thought he was halfway in love with Erin already. But that didn't solve her problem.

"Ryan, I think we need to go."

"I agree," he whispered, lowering his head again. His tongue dipped into her mouth as his lips molded to hers, drawing them into even greater intimacy. Lisa felt her breasts swell and tingle as they were pressed against his chest.

He lifted his head. "I think we'd better stop now, or I won't be able to keep my promise."

His warning brought an immediate agreement on Lisa's part. She pushed against his chest, trying to gain some breathing space. "I was right. This wasn't a good idea."

"Oh, it's been good, sweetheart," he murmured, teasing. "But I can't stand much more of this and remain sane."

"Well, it certainly wasn't my idea," she protested and backed out of his arms. "We'd better join Paul and Erin."

"You go ahead," he said, nodding toward the door. "I'll have to wait a few minutes or Paul is going to slug me."

His arousal was obvious, and Lisa nodded after only one look.

She turned abruptly for the door. She needed to get away from Ryan. He was drawing her back under his spell, as he did two years ago. But nothing had changed. He was still wealthy, living an entirely different kind of life from her. She stooped and picked up the cards, pencil, and paper she'd dropped and marched into the den.

"Ready to play?" she asked brightly, keeping her gaze on the cards as she took them from the box.

The other two were sitting on the same sofa when Lisa looked up and Erin had a look on her face that resembled what Lisa thought was on hers. Somehow she didn't think they'd occupied their time talking about cards.

"I'm ready," Erin said breathlessly. "Paul's a wonderful teacher. I'm sure I'll be able to play just fine. He explained everything to me."

Lisa recognized nervous talk when she heard it. After all, she exhibited the same difficulty a few times recently. Paul said nothing, staring across the room, a frown on his brow. Whatever had happened, it hadn't made him happy.

"Where's Ryan?" he suddenly asked.

Lisa willed her cheeks not to turn red. "Probably still in the kitchen talking to Mom," she blatantly lied. "Do you want me to go find him?"

"No. I'm sure he'll be along in a minute," Paul assured her.

Lisa sat down on the opposite sofa. "Are you and Erin going to be partners?" she asked, watching them.

Paul hesitated, then shrugged his shoulders. "Sure. Why not?"

She started shuffling the cards. "Then you need to come sit over here."

The door to the den opened and Ryan strolled in. "Did I keep you waiting? Margaret and I were talking about Frank," he said.

Lisa frowned. He could have thought of another topic, instead of using her father—unless he'd really talked to Margaret about Frank. She hoped he hadn't upset her.

Paul quickly moved over to the sofa by Lisa as Ryan came closer. His eyes narrowed suspiciously as Ryan gently touched her shoulder as he walked by. She kept her head down, watching her hands as she shuffled the cards.

"Who wants to keep score?" she asked, motioning to the paper and pencil. "Paul was a math major. Shall we trust him?"

The others murmured their agreement and she started dealing the cards.

"What are we playing to?" Ryan asked.

She looked up and saw a look in his eye that made her wonder what he was up to. After all, he'd looked the same way out in the hall just a few minutes ago.

"I don't suppose we're in a hurry to finish," she said, watching him. "How about five hundred? Or a thousand?"

"A thousand sounds good," Paul said.

"Oh, let's make it five hundred," Erin suggested. "It would take too long to get to a thousand."

Everyone seemed happy with that, and they started picking up their hands, arranging their cards.

"What are we playing for?"

Ryan's question surprised everyone.

"Are you talking about money?" Paul asked belligerently. "Think you don't have enough? You'll just fleece us as well?"

"Paul!" both Lisa and Erin protested.

"No, I'm not talking about money," Ryan replied calmly. "But it makes the game a lot more fun it we're playing for something."

"What do you suggest?" Lisa asked cautiously.

He pursed his lips, as if considering her question, but Lisa had a sneaky suspicion he'd already planned the prize.

"How about the losers have to do the supper dishes?" he offered, an innocent smile on his face.

"Oh, that's not bad," Erin said. "I would've offered anyway. It's only you two guys who wouldn't do them normally."

"We've offered," Paul said defensively. "Margaret usually shoos us out of the kitchen."

"Well, tonight, one of us will be stuck in the kitchen.

We'll just have to explain to Margaret." Ryan finished arranging his cards and looked across at Lisa. "Agreed?"

"I'm willing," she said and watched Ryan grin back at her. She was still suspicious.

They settled down to serious play. Paul's good humor seemed to have been restored, and he encouraged Erin, teaching her as they went.

"I think that might be called table talk," Ryan teased after Paul explained that Erin couldn't lead spades until they'd been played.

"No, that's a rule," Paul explained seriously.

"He knows, Paul. He's just teasing you," Lisa said.

"Oh. Well, Erin's just learning, anyway. It seems only fair to explain all the rules."

"I thought you would've done that before we started. You had a lot of time." Ryan's eyebrows shot up as both Erin and Paul turned bright red. He looked at Lisa and she shrugged.

"So, what are you going to lead, Erin?" Ryan quickly asked, studying his own cards.

She pulled out a card and laid it on the table, looking hopefully at Paul.

"Good choice, honey," he said, nodding, his mind on which card to play.

Ryan looked across at Lisa and mouthed the word *honey* with a question mark at the end. She frowned at him and shook her head. It wouldn't be a good idea to tease the other two right now.

"What is this?" Paul suddenly asked, staring at both of them. "Are you two signaling across the table?"

Ryan looked as if he was ready to explain what they'd been doing, but Lisa rushed in before he could. "No. Ryan was just—just teasing me. And *I* was trying to make him behave himself."

"Sounds like a tough job," Paul muttered. He played his card and looked at Ryan.

"Now you can play spades when it's your turn, Erin," Ryan said, "because I'm trumping your diamond."

"Does that mean I lose?" Erin asked, looking at Paul, her brows furrowed.

"Just that trick. It wasn't your fault, Erin," Paul assured his partner, and Ryan grinned at Lisa again.

The lead seesawed back and forth between the couples before Lisa and Ryan began to pull away. Paul's competitive spirit grew fierce, but he never took it out on Erin. His patience when she misplayed was more like that of the Paul Lisa knew rather than of the man he'd been the past few hours.

When Lisa and Ryan reached five hundred, it was already after one o'clock. Lisa suggested they stop playing and have lunch. "If Mom hasn't fixed anything, we can make sandwiches," she suggested.

"Fine," Paul agreed, a little down that he and Erin had lost.

"Now that Erin's getting the hang of it," Ryan said, "we can play again after lunch and give the two of you a chance to recoup your losses."

"You've got a deal," Paul said, his lips pressed together in determination.

"What will we play for next time?" Erin asked.

"Oh, we'll think of something," Ryan assured her, and Lisa felt sure whatever that something was, it had been Ryan's goal the entire time.

Subduing her curiosity, she stood. "I'll go check with Mom in the kitchen. Since she's working on tomorrow's dinner, why don't you wait here so we won't all get in her way?"

She left the others in the den and found her mother sitting at the table drinking a cup of coffee.

"Mom?"

Her mother looked around. "Have you finished playing cards? I looked in about half an hour ago, but you all looked deeply involved in the game, so I didn't disturb you.''

"Yes, everyone seemed to enjoy it. By the way, Erin and Paul will do the dishes after dinner this evening. That was what we played for.''

"What fun. Who's idea was that?'' Margaret asked, a smile on her face.

"Ryan's, of course. I think he's up to something, but I'm not sure what.''

"Whatever it is, it won't hurt anyone, I'm sure. He's a gentleman.''

Lisa studied her mother. She seemed quite content, more so then when the guests first arrived. "You're happy?'' she asked.

Margaret looked up, surprised. "Why, yes, dear. I've enjoyed having all of you here. I thought this fall that I was going to be too lonely, but now I know I like being alone.'' She grinned at Lisa. "Frankly, I like having an evening to myself and reading an hour or so before I go to sleep.''

"I've worried about your getting lonely.''

"Well, don't. I have several friends who are alone, too. We've formed a support group. I can call any of them if I need someone to talk to.''

Margaret's contentment made Lisa wonder if her mother would even *want* her to return to Dalhart, whether she lived with her mother or alone. But if she were pregnant, she knew she could count on her mother to help her. Now that she'd had time to think about the prospect, she thought she'd be disappointed if she wasn't carrying Ryan's child.

That might be all she would ever have of him in her life. And if she couldn't marry anyone else, why not have his child? She took a deep breath, wondering if she was going crazy.

"Is anything wrong, dear?'' Margaret asked, studying her.

"No, Mom. Actually, I came in to see about lunch. We're all getting hungry."

"I fixed a tray of cold cuts for sandwiches. It's all ready in the refrigerator."

"Aren't you going to eat with us?"

"No, I ate already. I need to go out and check on Betsy while I'm at a stopping place with the cooking. After you've finished lunch, I'll go back to work." She didn't seem the least bit disturbed about all she had to do. Lisa knew her mother enjoyed cooking.

"I'll go get the others. I made them wait in the den so we wouldn't bother you."

When she summoned the three others and the men learned Margaret was going to the barn, they both offered to go with her.

"Well, it might be a good idea if one of you did," Margaret said, "but there's no need for both of you to go outside."

"It was my fault Betsy got into the chicken feed," Ryan said. "I'll go with you."

Paul didn't protest but just shrugged his shoulders.

"We're having sandwiches for lunch. We'll get everything ready while you're gone," Lisa said. She watched as her mother and Ryan headed for the barn. Ryan seemed awfully pleased with the way things were working out. She wondered again just what he was up to.

When they reached the barn, Ryan shut the door behind them while Margaret went directly to the cow, still lying down in the shadows.

"Poor Betsy," she crooned, scratching the cow's forehead. "How are you feeling?"

"Margaret, did you think the storm is letting up a little?" Ryan asked.

"Oh, maybe a little. We'll listen to another weather report when we get back to the house. They have them every hour on the hour."

"How's Betsy?"

"Seems to be a little better. I think I'll try to get her to her feet." She took hold of the halter on the cow's head and tugged, calling to the cow as she did so.

"Want me to push?" Ryan asked from behind the cow.

"I don't think so. Sometimes, the result of overeating is, uh, rather messy at that end."

He took a quick step back. "Thanks for the warning."

After a minute, Betsy struggled to her feet and Margaret slowly led her around the barn. As she did so, she called to Ryan, "How are you and Lisa getting along?"

He looked sharply at her. "What do you mean?"

"Isn't that why you came? To see Lisa?"

"I said I came to see you and Frank," he reminded her.

"But you knew Lisa would be here."

He walked over to where she had stopped, letting Betsy take a breather. "Do you mind?" he asked, not bothering to deny her assumption.

"No. Frank and I both thought—no, hoped—you might work things out. But then Frank died and so much time passed by, I'd given up hope."

"I was angry at first, and confused." He paused before admitting what had hurt the most. "And she said she didn't love me."

Margaret started Betsy walking again and Ryan followed on the other side of the cow. "A good marriage takes a lot of work."

"I know. I didn't do a good job the first time. I got my priorities mixed up. But I promise you, if she'll give me another chance, I won't make the same mistake twice."

Margaret smiled. "I'm pulling for you."

"Then I figure I can't lose."

With Erin's help, it didn't take long to set everything out for lunch. Lisa kept listening for the others' return, but all she heard was the blowing storm. "When do you think the storm will start tapering off?"

"It seems a little less intense now than it was this morning," Paul said. He turned to stare at Erin, a sad look on his face, while she filled glasses with ice.

"It will seem strange to leave after all of us being together for so long," she said as she worked.

"Maybe after I come back to Dallas, we could have lunch together sometime," Lisa suggested. "On a Saturday, of course. I get only half an hour for lunch on school days."

"I'd love that," Erin said, turning to smile at her. "Paul could join us, too," she added.

He gave a noncommittal answer. "We'll see."

"Remind me to give you my phone number before you leave," Lisa said.

"Oh, that's all right. Ryan has it."

Her response surprised Lisa. Her number had been unlisted since her divorce. She opened her mouth to ask how he'd gotten it but then stopped. She didn't want to know.

She finally heard the back door open and close and hurried over to the connecting door. "Hi. Was Betsy doing all right?"

"She's better. We got her up and walking a little. I'll go back this evening and do it again," Margaret said, smiling at her daughter as she took off her coat.

"We've got everything ready for lunch, Ryan, as soon as you wash up."

"I'll be right with you. After petting Betsy, I'd better go upstairs and do a thorough job. Go ahead and fix your sandwiches."

Five minutes later, Lisa sat staring at her sandwich. She'd decided to wait for Ryan's return before eating so he wouldn't have to eat alone. Paul and Erin were halfway through their sandwiches while Margaret kept up a steady stream of talk.

She paused to turn to Lisa. "Dear, why don't you go

see if Ryan needs a towel or anything? He's been gone a long time.''

Paul looked up quickly and then rose. "I'll go."

"No, Paul," Lisa said, standing up. "Eat your sandwich and I'll be back in a minute." He still seemed to think she needed protection from Ryan. Lisa knew she only needed protection from herself.

She hurried through the cold hall and up the stairs. There was no sign of Ryan, but the bathroom door was closed. She tapped on it and called out his name.

The door was swung open so quickly she almost fell over. Ryan caught her against him and pulled her into the small room, closing the door behind her.

"I—I came to see if you needed a towel or anything."

"And I've been standing here waiting, hoping you'd come," he told her with a grin.

"I thought you were hungry," she said, growing breathless at the look in his eyes.

"Oh, I am, sweetheart, I am." Before she could answer, Ryan's lips captured hers, filling her with sweet longing. He ran his hands under her sweater, caressing her skin.

"Ryan, you've got to stop," she protested as he lifted his lips, struggling to remember why she needed to avoid his touch.

"I can't. I've got this theory, you see," he said, with that look in his eye.

Her hands lay on his chest, with the intent to push him away, but his words caught her interest. "What theory?"

"I think that the reason we never get around to talking is that I'm so hungry for you that I'm like a dieter who suddenly sees a candy bar. I can't take just one bite." One hand slipped down to caress her hips and press her more tightly against him.

She stirred, trying to concentrate on his words, but his body language was almost too powerful.

"Oh, really? What—what's the solution?"

"Frequent bites," he said softly, dipping down to gently nip her lips, "so I don't feel so deprived."

She moaned as he continued to nibble on her lips, her neck, her ears. Finally, frustration drove her to clasp his face in her hands and stretch up to meet his lips with hers. The kiss went on forever but ended too soon, leaving them both breathless.

Lisa swallowed, watching his mouth hungrily descend again. She said hurriedly, "Ryan, we've got to stop this. It's not right."

"Nothing has ever felt so right to me. We were always good together, sweetheart, and that hasn't changed."

His words hit her hard. "No, but neither has anything else," she whispered, "and that's why this isn't right."

When she pushed against his hard chest, he frowned and released her with a sigh. "Okay. You win this time."

Lisa led the way downstairs, but she wasn't happy with winning. It felt more like she was losing when she left his arms, just as it had when she'd divorced him.

THIRTEEN

Their delayed return to the kitchen upset only Paul. He gave each of them a hard stare, and what he saw didn't improve his disposition.

Ryan made himself a huge sandwich. "Going to the barn really worked up an appetite. Have you listened to the weather report yet, Margaret?" he asked before taking a bite of his sandwich.

"Oh, I forgot." She hurried over to the kitchen cabinet where she kept her battery-operated radio. When she turned it on, only music was heard. Checking her watch, she said, "It's a couple of minutes until they give another report."

"I thought the storm was lessening," Ryan commented. "But if it's going to end today, it ought to start slowing down a lot more."

No one had any comment. Lisa concentrated on her sandwich, though her appetite was gone. Sitting next to Ryan, all she could think about were those stolen moments in the bathroom. They both disturbed and excited her. She sighed.

"Tired?" Ryan murmured.

Looking into his eyes, she couldn't hold back a shudder. "No, just thinking."

"That's a dangerous occupation," he said, staring deeply into her eyes.

"Lisa, I think you and I should be partners this afternoon," Paul said abruptly.

It took her a minute to realize he was talking about cards, and her cheeks flushed. "Oh?"

Ryan studied the other man before saying, "Sure, that's okay with me if you think you can't win with Erin."

Lisa winced at the expression on Erin's face. Poor Erin. She didn't realize that Paul thought he was protecting Lisa.

"I meant no such thing!"

"That's all right, Paul. I understand," Erin assured him stiffly. "I'm just a beginner. If winning is so important to you, of course you should have Lisa as a partner." She rose from the table. "If you'll excuse me, I need to go upstairs."

"Damn it, that's not what I meant!" Paul shouted. He shoved his chair back from the table and followed her after sending a glare Ryan's way.

The swinging door gradually stilled before those left at the table said anything.

"Well, I think Paul's frustration may be growing," Ryan murmured. "Not an uncommon occurrence."

His teasing grin sent shivers down Lisa's spine. Ryan was right about that. Even though she knew she was falling back into the trap of letting her desires override her head, she seemed powerless to fight it. She was even questioning the wisdom of trying. Given the choice of a sterile existence, alone because no man but Ryan could satisfy her, she found herself leaning toward some kind of relationship with the man beside her.

He touched her cheek. "You haven't finished your sandwich."

"No, I lost my appetite." She drew away from his touch, undecided.

"I need to get something from my bedroom," Margaret suddenly announced, rising from the table. "I'll be back in a minute. Ryan, if they give the weather report before I get back, you be sure to listen to it."

"Right, Margaret," he murmured, but he was staring at Lisa.

As soon as the door swung to behind Margaret, he leaned over to Lisa. "Time for another nibble," he whispered.

She let his lips touch hers before resolving not to let him sway her again. "No, Ryan," she said, pulling back.

He stood and paced across the kitchen, before turning to face her. "What's the matter? You don't like me to touch you all of a sudden?"

Lisa stayed stubbornly silent. He moved back to her side, staring down at her. "Well?"

Standing, she said, "When you touch me, I forget too much. It's always been that way. That's why—why we made love yesterday. But there's got to be more than just you turning me on."

"There is more than that! I love you!" he shouted in frustration.

"You said you loved me when we married, too."

"I did!"

"But don't you see, Ryan? I loved you, too, but that still didn't make our marriage work out." She fought to keep the tears from falling.

"Because *you* left. You said you didn't love me anymore."

Lisa heard the anger in his voice and understood his pain. But if he'd known she loved him, he would never have let her leave. And if she'd stayed, she was afraid she would've eventually hated him and, even worse, hated herself. "I had to say that. I couldn't be what you wanted me to be." Tears slipped from her eyes and traced paths down her cheeks.

The music stopped and the announcer gave the latest

weather report, but the two in the kitchen didn't hear the words. They stared at each other, pain etched on their faces.

Paul and Erin stepped into the kitchen, seeking their fellow cardplayers. It took little perception for them to realize they'd interrupted an argument.

"Lisa!" Paul called, hurrying to her side. "Are you all right? What did he do to you?" He turned to glare at Ryan.

"Nothing," she gasped, grabbing Paul's arm as he moved toward Ryan. "We were just talking," she whispered.

Erin moved over beside the others. "Why don't we wait for them in the den, Paul?"

"Lisa, you should come to the den with us," Paul insisted, not budging a step.

Lisa realized the wisdom of Paul's words. The pain their talk had brought hurt too much. She nodded and moved toward the door, but she couldn't resist a look at Ryan. Her eyes were filled with sorrow. "I'm sorry, Ryan," she muttered.

His gaze blazed back at her. "Not half as much as I am."

She swallowed and managed to walk away from him. Moving past the other two without looking at them, Lisa headed to the den.

When Ryan finally entered the den, he found three unhappy people awaiting him, which matched his mood exactly. He'd messed up. He'd thought he could charm Lisa back into his bed and work out the difficulties later. One of the things he'd always admired about her, however, was her intelligence. She wasn't going to be swayed by that kind of behavior even if she did want him.

The only solace he found in what had happened was that she'd admitted she loved him. Unfortunately, she'd also said it wasn't enough.

"What did the weather report say?" Erin asked as he entered.

Ryan shrugged his shoulders. "I missed it. Margaret came back to the kitchen and said she'd let us know when she heard the next one."

There was an awkward silence, and Ryan studied the other three. Lisa and Erin were sitting on one couch, with Paul alone on the other. He asked, "Are we ready to play cards again?"

Though everyone agreed, there wasn't a lot of enthusiasm. Ryan decided he should give up his scheme. In fact, he thought it would be for the best. His idea of being alone with Lisa in short doses wasn't working for either one of them. She was growing angry and he was growing frustrated.

"Who's going to be my partner?" He looked at Paul for an answer. If he wasn't going to go ahead with his plan, it didn't really matter who his partner was. He could enjoy watching Lisa whether she was his partner or not.

"We'll keep the same partners," Paul finally said. "Erin and I will win this time."

They all settled in the correct places, and Ryan looked at Lisa. He thought she'd never looked lovelier in spite of the fact that she refused to look at him. Although she'd rejected him, he still responded to her beauty. Even in the thick sweater she wore, he could warm his thoughts on her curves, as long as he kept them under control.

Not easy to do.

Paul shuffled the cards and dealt them around the table. As they gathered them up, Erin asked, "What are we playing for this time? More dishes?"

Ryan tried to fight the temptation. He really did. But time alone with Lisa was too much to turn down when it was offered. He promised himself he'd behave. Clearing his throat, he said, "Well, the only other chore we do is tend to the animals. I suppose the losers could take care of the barn chores in the morning."

"What fun!" Erin exclaimed, her face brightening. "I could even look forward to losing. Gathering the eggs was great."

Ryan understood the frustration on Paul's face. Trapped by his partner's enthusiasm and the hurt he would deal her if he opposed the idea, he glared at Ryan. He could only shrug his shoulders in return. If he and Lisa lost, he would get uninterrupted time in the barn. Though after their conversation in the kitchen, he knew he shouldn't be alone with her.

If *they* won, then Paul and Erin would be out of the house for half an hour. And he knew Margaret wouldn't interrupt their time together. He'd at least be able to talk to Lisa. Either way, he couldn't lose. Unless he lost control.

His gaze met Lisa's across the coffee table. Her awareness of him was evident in her face, but she didn't offer any encouragement for his plan. But then, she didn't oppose it either. His eyes dwelled on her soft red lips until his body began reacting to his thoughts. He'd better concentrate on his cards.

Tension grew as they played. Paul seemed determined to lose. But Ryan thought his competitive nature made his decision difficult. Erin grew confused. She finally complained when Paul trumped her lead.

"But that trick was already mine. Why did you do that, Paul?"

"Sorry. I wasn't thinking."

Lisa shook her head at Ryan, warning him not to say anything. She was right. Even though Paul's histrionics weren't necessary, at least not now, the man was trying to be a friend to Lisa. He was being punished enough for his gallantry without Ryan's adding to it.

They played on, the game going on longer than in the morning because the men began making preposterous bids and then going in the hole, reversing their scores.

It was a relief when Margaret stuck her head in the door. "The latest report says the storm will end late this evening. They hope to have the roads open in twenty-four hours. Does anyone need anything to eat or drink?''

Lisa jumped up from the table. "I'll fix coffee for everyone, Mom. I think we need a break. Ryan, would you help me carry the tray?''

When Paul began to offer in his place, Lisa sent him a glare that would've shriveled a cactus. He subsided back against the cushions.

Ryan followed Lisa from the room, knowing she didn't have a romantic interlude in mind. The look in her eyes was one she used on a recalcitrant student, he was sure. It was very effective.

Once the door closed behind them, she whirled around, her hands on her hips. "Ryan Hall, what do you think you're doing?''

With a hangdog manner that didn't quite hide a smile, he said meekly, "I don't know, Mrs. Hall.''

"Ms. McGregor!" she corrected, frowning severely, though he thought the corners of her lips quivered. Her sense of humor was one of the delightful things about her.

"Yes, ma'am," he muttered, still hanging his head.

"Oh, stop acting that way. You're not fooling me," she said, shoving against his chest.

He captured her hand there. "You always were too smart for me, Ms. McGregor." The warm look he gave her had her backing away from him.

"Ryan, you have to stop . . ." she hesitated as he moved toward her.

"Stop what, Ms. McGregor?" he asked. He fought the urge to pull her into his arms.

Lisa, however, wasn't fooled by his innocent act this time. "Stop trying to lose. I'm not going to let you make love to me in the barn or anywhere else. I made that mistake once, but I won't again." She pressed her lips firmly together and stared at him.

What could he say? To deny that that had been his

original intent would be a lie. To tell her he'd changed his mind would be fruitless. He shrugged.

"When we go back in there, I want you to try to win."

"Yes, ma'am," he agreed. He put his hands in his pockets, out of temptation's way, but his eyes were filled with the desire he felt every time he got near her.

A shudder wracked her body and Ryan hoped she was having as much difficulty with her self-control as he was.

"Now, let's go fix the coffee," she muttered.

"You mean you really intend to fix coffee? I thought you just wanted to get me all to yourself." His ridiculous words drew a sigh from Lisa.

"In the kitchen," she commanded, her marine sergeant air undermined by her lips quivering with a quickly suppressed smile.

"Yes, ma'am," he repeated, following her through the door.

Margaret had already put on water for coffee and was filling a tray with coffee mugs. "Want some brownies to go with the coffee? I made a batch a little while ago."

"You mean they're still warm?" Ryan asked, his eyes lighting up.

"Yes, just as you like them," Margaret said.

It amazed Lisa that her mother remembered so much from Ryan's short visit when they were married. He'd been particularly fond of her brownies served warm. Lisa couldn't help wondering if her mother was trying to encourage Ryan.

Margaret added a plate of brownies and napkins to the tray. As soon as the kettle whistled, she poured hot water into each of the cups and stirred. "There. I think that's everything."

Lisa leaned over and kissed her mother's cheek. "And that means go away and don't bother me," she said to Ryan.

"Lisa! I never said that."

"I know, Mom. But that's what we're going to do. If

I can convince Ryan to behave himself." She cast a reproving look at him.

"I swear I'm innocent," he said to Margaret.

"Not guilty, maybe. Innocent, never," Margaret teased in return.

"Margaret! You've wounded me!"

"Stop playacting, you two," Lisa admonished, though she couldn't keep from smiling. It was good to see her mother happy. "Pick up the tray, Ryan, before the coffee gets cold and we have to make more explanations to Paul. I haven't been so closely watched since I was sixteen and had my first boyfriend. I thought Dad wouldn't let us out of his sight."

"He didn't want to," Margaret said dryly.

"Neither does Paul," Ryan said, doing as Lisa asked and picking up the tray. "Lead on, *ma commandante*. Let's go feed the poor savages in the wilderness."

"You're more interested in feeding those brownies to yourself. I know you!" Lisa teased, the tension fading somewhat as they left the kitchen.

Ryan immediately turned her stomach into more complicated knots. A serious look on his face, he stopped, the tray in his hands, and said, "No, you don't know me at all, or you'd know I want more than sex from you, Lisa."

"I know that you married the wrong woman for what you want," she responded, looking away and folding her arms across her chest.

"You're wrong, Lisa. I married the only woman in the world for me."

She stared at him, her eyes full of longing, before she turned and opened the door to the den. Her only words were spoken to the two waiting inside. "Mom made brownies for us."

Two hours later, the game was finally drawing to a close. Whether Lady Luck was rewarding Ryan's good behavior or he was more skillful at losing than Lisa realized, she and her partner were down seventy-eight points. Erin and Paul's score was 476. Even if Paul made the minimum bid of one, Erin was sure to bid more than two and they would win the game.

Lisa had to give Ryan credit. He'd stopped throwing hands, making stupid plays, even making ridiculous bids. As far as she could tell, he'd just played the cards he'd gotten. And since he only dealt the cards every fourth hand, he couldn't even be blamed for the rotten cards he'd received.

Paul, on the other hand, seemed to attract a large number of spades, several aces every hand, and a lot of other face cards. Try as he might, he couldn't avoid winning.

As he arranged his last hand, Lisa heard him mutter a quiet "damn" under his breath. She smiled at him, trying to let him know his vigilance wasn't necessary. However, he refused to take the hint.

Erin urged her partner on. "Come on, Paul, with even a halfway decent hand, we can win. I want to be able to say I won."

"Fine," he finally said. "I bid six."

"Paul!" Erin complained. "You're overbidding again. I want to win!"

"You bid your hand and I'll bid mine," he growled.

Lisa stared at her own cards and thought he might not be overbidding. Her highest card was a jack and she had only one spade. *Someone* had an outstanding hand.

When the game was ended, Paul was vindicated, having taken almost every trick. Thrilled with winning for the first time, Erin threw herself across the low coffee table and kissed Paul on the lips. "Thank you, partner. That was great!"

"Not a bad reward," Ryan murmured, a wicked smile on his face. He eyed Lisa speculatively.

"You didn't win," she reminded him.

"That's debatable."

Erin plopped back down on the sofa beside Ryan and

leaned back against the cushions with a sigh. "I'm exhausted. That was tense work."

Lisa grinned. Erin hadn't been half as tense as Paul. Poor thing, he must be exhausted. "There's half a brownie left to restore your energy."

"Oh, no. I can't. I pigged out on those earlier. I won't be able to eat any dinner if I have that, too. Paul? You want it?"

"No, thank you," he murmured stiffly.

Erin ignored her partner's ill humor. "How about you, Ryan?" As he reached for it, she added, "Though you certainly had your fair share earlier, too."

"You can't ever get enough of Margaret's brownies. By the way, Lisa, can you make them?"

"Yes," she murmured, ignoring the lazy smile on his face as he sprawled out, at ease.

"She's made them for me," Paul asserted. In contrast, he leaned forward, resting his forearms on his knees, a frown on his face.

"I can make peanut brittle," Erin bragged, watching Paul.

"Paul loves peanut brittle. Maybe you should make him some to thank him for teaching you to play spades," Lisa suggested to Erin. "When we go to lunch, you could present him with your efforts."

"All right, I will." Erin nodded her thanks to Lisa and shot a grin to Paul, inviting him to join in the fun.

"What lunch? Have you been making plans without me?" Ryan asked.

"Lisa and I were going to get together for lunch one Saturday after we got back to Dallas. Then I invited Paul to join us."

Before Ryan could ask to be invited, Erin suddenly shouted, "I've got it!"

"What have you got?" Ryan asked in amusement.

"Instead of lunch, we can get together for another

spades competition. I'll have all of you over and serve my famous peanut brittle."

Lisa said nothing, but she vowed to be busy whenever Erin called. She didn't need the strain of more time spent with Ryan.

Paul fiddled with the stack of playing cards. "I doubt your parents would like that."

"Why not?" Erin asked, a puzzled look on her face.

"They'd probably prefer that you and Ryan entertain more influential people than a couple of schoolteachers."

The enthusiastic glow on Erin's face faded and she glared at Paul. "My parents are not snobs. Besides, I have my own place and can invite anyone I want."

"Don't worry, Paul. If you won't go to Erin's, come to my place," Ryan said, laughing. "I'm definitely not a snob."

Before Lisa could help herself, she muttered, "No, but your mother is." She immediately clapped her hand to her mouth, as if she could recapture the words. Then, realizing the futility of her movement, she took her hand down and said, "I'm sorry, Ryan. I shouldn't have said that."

"Why not? It's no less than the truth," he said, smiling at her.

"But I shouldn't have said it," she repeated stubbornly.

"Mother defends her social position like those ladies who marry a famous name and defend its star status even though they had nothing to do with earning it." He looked at Lisa intently. "I never explained Mother to you because I didn't think about it. I just assumed you'd know. Another of my wrong assumptions."

Erin, seemingly unaware of how important Ryan's words were to Lisa, added another blow to her perceptions. "It doesn't matter much what Mrs. Hall thinks anyway. She doesn't live with Ryan anymore."

FOURTEEN

Lisa stared at Ryan, surprised.

He returned her stare with a steady smile.

"Shouldn't I have said anything?" Erin asked. "I didn't realize it was a secret."

"It's not," Ryan drawled. "I just haven't had a chance to catch up on things with Lisa." And he wasn't about to discuss his failed marriage in front of Paul. There were a lot of things he wanted to ask her, but now wasn't the time.

He'd only lived with his mother for convenience. Their family home was large, with a competent staff. His mother hadn't interfered with his life much until he married. Then, he'd figured he and Lisa would look for a house. But he couldn't do that right away. He'd assumed Lisa would understand the arrangement wasn't forever. And he *had* assumed their marriage was.

Big mistake.

"Wonder if the storm has died down any," he said, rising to stroll over to the window.

"Well?" Erin asked, since no one else said anything.

"Maybe a little. I still wouldn't want to be out in it."

"I wish the electricity would come back on," Erin murmured, leaning her head back against the sofa again.

"Why?" Lisa finally asked. Her gaze remained pinned to the man by the window.

"I'd like to see the lights on the tree again. I think we did a terrific job."

Lisa reluctantly turned from staring at Ryan to look up at the tree. "Yes, it's beautiful . . . except for the bare spot on top."

"I hope you find the star," Erin said, smiling sympathetically at Lisa.

"Thanks. I was only two when we bought it," Lisa said, a faraway look in her eyes. "Mom said I picked it out only because it was the biggest and the brightest." She laughed. "Dad said I chose it because I always knew what was the most expensive."

Erin laughed with her. "My dad says things like that, too. I think it's required to complain about a daughter's expenses."

"I know," Lisa agreed. "He teased me a lot. But when I needed him, he was always there. Sometimes, I'd see him watching me and I'd think I was doing just fine. The next thing I knew, he'd be picking up the pieces, giving me confidence to go on."

She stared blindly up at the top of the tree. "I miss him . . . all the time." Her throat ached with the unshed tears.

"I can't imagine not having my father around," Erin said. "He's always there for me."

"That'll make it hard for your husband," Paul suggested.

"What do you mean?"

He shrugged his shoulders. "Sometimes a woman expects her husband to do everything her father did for her, with a lot less experience or money. The husband would lose that competition every time."

While Erin hotly contested Paul's assertion, Lisa returned her gaze to Ryan only to find him staring at her.

Had she done that? Had she expected Ryan to meet her every need as her father had done?

She hoped not, but she wasn't sure. Her parents had been wonderfully supportive, but her father had done even more. Ryan wouldn't know her needs as her father had done. Frank had had twenty-two years to understand her. Ryan had had only ten weeks.

Looking away, she closed her eyes, adding that thought to the others that were piling up to make her question her behavior. Erin's voice distracted her.

"I don't think I'll be that way. I'll deal with a husband when I get one, but I'm glad to have my father still around." She paused before adding, "Ryan's father died five years ago."

Paul looked over at Ryan, frowning. "You must have been pretty young when he died."

"Twenty-four, a year older than Lisa was when Frank died." He gave a wry smile. "I thought I knew it all. I'd just gotten my MBA, but I was still wet behind the ears. I took over the company he'd spent his life building and almost lost it two years later."

"But you've been wonderfully successful since then," Erin said encouragingly.

"Yeah. And every day it's a tribute to my father rather than my supposed genius." He shrugged.

"I'm going to give my dad a hug as soon as I see him," Erin finally said. "And my mom, too. This Christmas is teaching me to appreciate things I've taken for granted."

"Yeah," Paul muttered noncommittally and stared at Erin. When she returned his gaze, he looked down at his hands.

"Maybe," Lisa began, almost in a whisper, "that's what Christmas is really about." She stared up at the bare spot on the tree. "Maybe it's about learning more about ourselves, about new beginnings, maybe even making amends."

Ryan moved over to stand beside her chair. "And forgivenesss. I think that's a part of Christmas, too."

Lisa nibbled on her bottom lip. He was right, of course. But she'd already forgiven him. Realizing her share of the guilt, she could do no less. That didn't solve their problem, though. She was still the country girl from the Panhandle, and he was still the wealthy man from Dallas.

Paul stood up, walking away from the Christmas tree. "Let's not get all dewy-eyed just because it's Christmas. In a couple of days, Christmas will be over. Then we've got to get through the rest of the year."

"Is your middle name Scrooge?" Erin demanded, trying to tease him out of his cynicism.

"Sure, why not? Sometimes I think he got a bad rap." When Erin would've protested, he held up his hand. "Just think about it. Christmas is just like those New Year's resolutions. Lots of promises that aren't carried out. We can't be Santa Claus every day of the year."

"But what about dreams?" Erin protested.

Lisa got up and moved to Paul's side, placing a hand on his arm. "Paul's not really that hard, Erin. He's just— just down a little today." She smiled up at him. "When we were decorating the tree and I began to remember those special times with my parents, I think I discovered the importance of all this. It's the magical times that get us over the rough ones. If we didn't have anything wonderful to remember, to look forward to, we couldn't survive the disasters."

Even Paul had nothing to say. Lisa smiled tremulously. "Enough philosophizing. Let's go see if Mom needs any help with dinner. I'm starving."

Everyone willingly headed to the kitchen. In response to Lisa's offer of their collective assistance, Margaret turned them down.

"No, I don't need any help. I made meat loaf and it's in the oven. Just set the table."

"Did you ever hear a new weather report?" Paul asked.

"Yes, they gave one a few minutes ago. It still says the storm should end soon. But the snow is deeper than they thought and they may not get the roads cleared off before Christmas day." Margaret had her back turned to them and didn't see Erin's face fall.

"Oh. I was hoping we'd be with my family on Christmas day."

It was Paul who reached out to comfort her. "Maybe they'll still get them open."

"When the storm stops and we find out how long it will take, we'll call the airport in Amarillo and see about flying the rest of the way," Ryan offered.

"What would you do with your car?" Paul asked.

"Leave it there. I can fly back into Amarillo and drive it home."

Lisa hoped she was already back in Dallas by then. She didn't want to tempt fate into bringing Ryan for another visit when she wouldn't have the others around for protection.

"One thing I will miss," Paul said as they ate their dinner, "other than the good company, of course, is your cooking, Margaret. If you ever want to move to Dallas, call me, not Lisa. I need you."

"Maybe I should just open a cooking school for bachelors," Margaret suggested with a laugh.

"Not a bad idea," Ryan said. "If you want me to finance it, I'll be glad to do so, as long as I get to attend free."

"Mom, you could do that next summer. Offer a week's cooking school for bachelors in June. If you got a list of graduating seniors in high school and college and mailed a brochure to their families, I'll bet you'd be overwhelmed with responses." Lisa got more excited as she thought about it. "You could give them a choice of weeks, doing it twice. If you stayed with me, you'd only have to pay rent for the kitchen you'd use for classes."

"You could probably work out something with the high

school," Paul contributed. "They have a great new setup, just installed last year."

"I'd love teaching the classes, but I don't think I'd like all the paperwork, writing the brochure, getting it mailed." Margaret seemed unconcerned with the excitement her daughter felt.

"But, Mom, it's a great idea."

"If she had someone who would handle all the details, maybe she'd consider it," Ryan suggested.

Lisa shook her head regretfully. "Not me. I'm too overloaded now. I couldn't do anything until school is out and by then it'd be too late."

"I could do all those things," Erin said slowly. "We could be partners, Margaret. I could even back you financially. It would be my first business venture."

Margaret's eyes lit up as Erin continued to discuss the idea. Soon she and Erin were tossing ideas back and forth, with Paul giving them his opinion as a bachelor. Lisa and Ryan exchanged amused glances and began clearing the table. The others scarcely noticed what they were doing.

When Lisa turned on the water at the sink, Erin objected. "You can't do the dishes tonight, Lisa. We lost that first game, remember?"

"But you and Mom and Paul have a lot to discuss. I don't want to stymie my mother's new career."

"Part of the curriculum has to be a quick cleanup. We'll discuss strategy with Margaret, and Paul and I will practice what she preaches." Erin came over to the sink and gently shoved Lisa away. "You and Ryan go into the den and entertain yourselves."

Paul joined Erin, bringing the last of the dishes with him. "Unless Ryan wants to contribute his opinion as a bachelor."

"I'm a bachelor with a housekeeper. Mother may have moved out, but I wasn't about to try to manage on my own."

"Then we don't need you. How to order dinner just won't be in the curriculum."

"Well, actually, I think we ought to include places with good takeouts and how to serve the food as if you'd cooked it," Margaret said, frowning.

"But that's sneaky," Erin said, grinning.

"Of course," Margaret agreed, smiling serenely.

Everyone laughed.

"Okay. We'll leave you to your planning. If you need us, just give us a call," Ryan offered, even as he pushed Lisa ahead of him out into the hall.

They walked into the den, and Lisa almost panicked as Ryan closed the door behind him. Lisa distanced herself from him, expecting him to try to draw her into his arms. Instead, he walked past her to put another log on the fire. After he'd done so, he stared down at the flames as if she weren't in the room.

Wondering what had caused the change in him, Lisa cautiously moved to the sofa and sat down, waiting. She wasn't at all sure being alone with him was a smart idea. When he finally turned around to look at her, he smiled ruefully and echoed her thoughts.

"I've been scheming for time alone with you, but now that we've got the entire evening, it's too much. I don't dare trust myself if I get too close."

Lisa wanted to tell him she didn't trust herself either if he got too close, if their kisses evolved into something more exciting. But she couldn't. They'd both be better off if she didn't share that information with him.

"Why don't you tell me about the negotiations that expanded your business two summers ago?" she asked, thinking about his earlier comments in the den. "I don't think I listened much at the time. I'd like to hear now."

"You're sure? I might bore you to death."

"No, you won't."

With a longing gaze at the empty spot beside her, he moved to the other sofa. Sitting down, he started his story a few weeks before their meeting, explaining how the actual negotiations were the culmination of earlier preparation, how he'd felt the expansion was an affirmation of what his father had done. Lisa began to understand that it was their meeting and subsequent marriage, not the negotiations, that interrupted things.

"We completed our agreement the day—" he paused, looking at her, "the day you told me you wanted a divorce."

"Oh, Ryan," she sighed. "I'm sorry."

He shrugged. "Your turn, now. Fill me in on a teacher's life. Other than the fact that I once attended high school, I don't know much about it."

Lisa talked about teaching to her heart's content, with Ryan giving her his complete attention. She discussed her frustrations and her triumphs equally. As she remembered funny happenings in her class, she strove to bring a smile to Ryan's face. She loved hearing his laughter.

"You should write a book, sweetheart," he told her after one story.

"Maybe one day I will."

The door opened and Erin and Paul entered.

"Enjoying yourselves?" Paul asked, looking first at Lisa and then Ryan.

"Yes, as a matter of fact, we are," Ryan said, sending a smile Lisa's way.

"What were you doing?" Erin asked before Paul frowned at her. "I mean, well—"

"It's okay, Erin. We've been talking," Lisa assured her, relieving her embarrassment. "Did you really make plans with Mom?"

"Yes. It's going to be terrific. She worked out a terrific curriculum in no time. She really knows her subject."

"Yes. I hope she'll go through with it. I think it would be good for her."

"It will be good for all of us," Paul assured her.

"You, too?"

"Right. I'm part of our little company."

"Company? You've certainly worked fast. You were in the kitchen for—" Lisa looked at her watch. "Good heavens, you've been talking for over two hours. And so have we," she said, looking at Ryan in surprise.

"It seemed like only a few minutes," he replied.

She agreed, her mind dwelling on him rather than on her mother's plans. They'd talked longer tonight than they ever had while they were married.

"Erin says she'll talk to her father and ask him to recommend a lawyer to draw up papers for us. We want everything to be clearly spelled out," Paul said, his face serious.

"No need for that," Ryan said. "I've got a couple of lawyers who work for me. They don't have enough to do. You can get them to draw up whatever papers you need."

"We don't need charity," Paul replied, shadows of his earlier belligerence in his voice.

Ryan nodded. "Of course not. But Margaret is—was my mother-in-law. If I want to help her, I don't think you should object to it."

"I didn't mean—thanks," Paul finally said.

"Good. I'll bring them over to meet you."

Erin chattered on about their plans, with Paul adding his own enthusiasm until Lisa stifled a yawn.

"Sorry. That's no reflection on your plans. It's just been a long day," she said. "Where's Mom, by the way?"

"Oh, I forgot. She wanted to see you in the kitchen," Erin said. "I'm sorry. I got distracted."

"Don't worry about it. I'll go now. If it had been urgent, she would've come and gotten me."

Lisa found her mother sitting at the kitchen table, pen in hand, working on her curriculum for their idea. "You don't have to do it all in one night, Mom."

"No, of course not, dear. I was just jotting down some ideas. I'm excited about this course."

"I'm glad."

"If we got a tremendous response, you might want to teach a class or two yourself. After all, you're almost as good a cook as me."

"We'll see," Lisa said. It was hard to think of giving up her summer to more teaching. She needed a break by June. "I won't leave you stranded if you need me."

"Good," her mother said and started writing something else down on her paper.

"Is that why you wanted to see me?" Lisa asked.

"Oh, no! I'd forgotten that I asked Erin to send you in." Margaret laid down her pen. "Dear, it's Christmas."

When she paused, Lisa grinned. "Yes, Mom, I know."

"Don't be silly, dear, of course you know. But I wanted to talk to you about presents. I bought a gift for Paul, of course, but not for Erin and Ryan since I didn't know they would be here. I wondered if you'd mind my giving Erin one of your gifts?"

"Of course not, Mom. But I'm sure they don't expect anything."

"That's the nicest part about giving gifts. Besides, Christmas is a time of new beginnings. This past year, I felt like I was marking time, waiting to die."

Lisa gasped and Margaret waved away her concern.

"I don't mean I was suicidal, dear, just—waiting." She sighed. "Anyway, having all of you here at Christmas has awakened me. Now I have a lot to look forward to."

"I'm glad, Mom," Lisa said, reaching out to clasp her hand. She'd intended Paul's presence to have that effect, but she hadn't planned on Ryan and Erin.

"So, I want to express my appreciation to them. That's why I want to give them gifts."

"All right, what do you have planned?" Lisa asked with a smile, trying to match her mother's enjoyment.

"Well, I bought you one of those makeup sets that are so nice. We can pick you up another one when we go into Amarillo next week. I thought Erin would like it."

"I'm sure she will, Mom. But what about the guys?"

"I bought Paul a nice leather shaving bag," Margaret said slowly, "but I don't have anything for Ryan. I've been thinking about it, and I've come up with an idea." She twirled the pen around on the paper, not looking at Lisa.

Lisa captured her mother's restless fingers. "What is it, Mom? I'm sure I won't object."

"I thought I'd give Ryan the sweater I knitted for your father last year." Margaret peeped from under her lashes at Lisa.

Lisa stood up and walked over to the kitchen counter, leaning against it. Her mother had finished the sweater for her father just before his heart attack. She'd folded it and kept it in her bedroom, a talisman, like the silver star, to keep her husband near. "Are you sure, Mom? Ryan won't mind if he doesn't get a present."

"There's no reason to just let it rot away. And Ryan has contributed to my Christmas as much as any of you. I've enjoyed seeing him again."

Lisa smiled to relieve her mother's anxious expression. "I think that's a nice idea. The blue will look great on Ryan."

Margaret smiled in relief. "Good. Actually, he and your father look somewhat alike."

Lisa stared at her mother in surprise. She'd never thought of that, though they were both tall and dark. But it wasn't comfort she got from Ryan's nearness.

Margaret interrupted her thoughts. "I suspect that's why you chose Paul. Because he's the opposite of Ryan in looks and everything else."

Lisa blinked. "Well, he's blond, Mom, but I don't think I really thought about that."

"Maybe not. Anyway, I like the idea of giving Ryan Frank's sweater. You know how much your dad liked him."

"Yes," Lisa whispered. The fact that Ryan and her father had taken to each other had made telling her father about her divorce doubly difficult. The two men had talked on the phone several times a week.

She walked back over to the table and gave her mother a hug. "You're right. Dad would be happy."

"Well," Margaret said briskly after hugging Lisa, "now that that's settled, all we have to do is wrap the gifts and put them under the tree after the others have gone to sleep."

"Won't that be rather difficult since we're all sleeping in the same room with the tree?"

"Hmmm. Why don't you go in and start getting the beds ready? I'm sure the others will take the hint and get ready for bed. I'll go up and put the presents out on my bed. When you come back in, bring the box of wrapping paper and ribbons by the TV set."

Lisa thought her mother would make a good general. She planned for Lisa to be the last to use the bath and bring the presents down to the kitchen. She'd join her there and they could wrap them quickly. Then, when she got up in the morning, before everyone else, she'd slip them under the tree.

"Then you'd better not sleep in the middle of the bed," Lisa suggested.

"No, I won't. You know what to do?" Margaret asked, her face as serious as if they were on a dangerous mission.

"What's going on in here?" Ryan asked, standing in the doorway behind them.

FIFTEEN

Margaret turned to look at Ryan. "It's Christmas. You're not supposed to ask questions like that."

Ryan's brows rose and he looked at Lisa. "She's expecting Santa Claus?"

"Well, it *is* Christmas." Lisa smiled at the pleasure on her mother's face. "Is everything all right in the den?" she asked Ryan.

"Sure, except I'm bored. Those two are discussing their new company. I hope you're as enthusiastic as they are, Margaret, because there's no way you can escape now."

"I don't want to, Ryan. For the first time since Frank's death, I have a lot of things to look forward to, thanks to all of you." She rose and pressed a kiss on Ryan's cheek. Before he could respond, she was at the door. "I'm sending the others to the bathroom. It's time we all got to bed. Tomorrow will be a big day."

"She really is feeling better?" Ryan asked.

"Yes," Lisa assured him as her eyes filled with tears. "Thanks to all of you. I guess I should've come home this year, but I didn't realize—it's like Sleeping Beauty's castle. The rest of the world passed by without either of us noticing this past year."

"Is this where I offer to awaken you with a kiss?" Ryan said, watching her.

She fought the urge to run. "I think you've already tried that," she reminded him.

"And did it work?"

More than she ever wanted to admit. His kiss had shown her she had no future with Paul. In fact, she had no future with any man except the one watching her. "You'd better go get in line for the bathroom."

"You didn't answer my question."

"We're not living in a fairy tale, Ryan. This is real life. Problems can't be solved with a kiss." But she wished they could. She wished she could melt into his arms and forget the world.

The kitchen door swung open and Paul entered. "Is it okay if I have a glass of milk, Lisa?"

"Sure, Paul. I'll pour it for you. Where's Erin?" Lisa said, grateful for the interruption. Ryan stood against the wall, watching her, a frown on his face, as she poured Paul's milk and handed it to him.

"Your mother sent her up for her turn in the bathroom. Margaret would make a great drill sergeant." Though he smiled before taking a sip of milk, Lisa could see his frustration.

"Sorry, Paul. She forgets we're not her students."

"That's what happens when you live alone," Ryan commented, moving over to lean on the counter by Lisa. "You forget how to live with other people."

"Some of us never knew," Lisa murmured, slanting a look at him from the corner of her eye.

"What's that supposed to mean?" he demanded immediately.

"Hey, if this is a private argument, I can—"

"No!" Lisa assured Paul.

"Yes," Ryan said just as quickly.

"Who's next?" Erin sang out as she entered the room.

"Through already?" Paul asked. "Did Margaret check behind your ears?"

Erin stared at him, not understanding.

"Paul, if Mom is really bothering you that much, I'll say something to her," Lisa said.

"No, don't mind me. I was just trying to harass Erin. She and Margaret think alike." Without another word, Paul moved past Erin, who still could think of nothing to say.

"What's wrong with him?" she finally asked as the door swung from his exit. "Except when we were discussing our new company, he's been a grouch all evening."

"Maybe all this togetherness is getting on his nerves," Lisa suggested.

"Or maybe he's frustrated as hell," Ryan added under his breath.

"What?" Erin asked, looking at him, puzzled.

Lisa shoved away from the cabinet, away from the man beside her. "Nothing, Erin. He didn't say anything. Come on, help me get the beds ready. I've a feeling Mom will have us up at the crack of dawn tomorrow."

They left Ryan in the kitchen.

Sometime in the darkest early-morning hours, something awakened Lisa. Her eyes opened slowly, regretting whatever urged them, and she raised up on one elbow. It took her a moment to recognize what she was hearing. Silence. Except for the crackle of the logs on the fire and her mother's gentle snores, there was no noise.

The storm had ended.

When they'd gone to bed that evening, it had raged on, proving the weathermen wrong again. Lisa had gotten so used to its howling winds, the stillness had pulled her from sleep.

Erin would be pleased. She was anxious to join her family for Christmas. Paul, too, seemed ready for their house party to end. His patience had disappeared.

And Ryan? How would be feel about their release? Lisa didn't know, any more than she understood her own reaction. Part of her was relieved that she wouldn't be confronted with her past, with the attraction Ryan always held for her. But another part of her didn't want him to leave. Ever.

She shoved back the covers and padded over to the window in her socks. The drifts of pure snow, under the gleam of a half-moon peeking from behind the clouds, were beautiful. One could almost forget the difficulties of gettting anywhere when it created such beauty.

A shiver raced through her and she moved away from the coldness of the outside that seeped through the glass. Making as little noise as possible, she added several logs to the slowly dying fire. Then she tiptoed to the door and slipped into the hallway. She might as well add her mother's presents to the tree now while everyone slept.

Several minutes later, she crept back into the room with the presents she and her mother had speedily wrapped in the kitchen after the others had gone to bed. Her mother's enthusiasm had increased, if anything. Lisa only hoped the others appreciated their gifts.

"Funny, you don't look like Santa Claus," Ryan whispered, startling her.

She juggled the presents, almost dropping them. Once she had them under control, she whispered back, "And you don't look like a good little boy, either. Go to sleep, or you'll get nothing."

Slipping the presents under the tree, she moved back to the sofa bed.

"The storm stopped."

His tone was noncommittal, but Lisa wondered what he was thinking. "Yes," she replied, offering none of her thoughts either.

"Erin will be pleased."

"Yes."

He said nothing as she slid beneath the covers, trying

not to disturb the other two women. As she settled down, he whispered, "Good night, Lisa."

"Good night, Ryan."

She wondered if she'd ever say those words to him again.

They awakened to a new world. Bright sunshine flooded the house, gleaming through the rows of icicles already forming along the edges of the roof. A clear blue sky completed the Christmas card—perfect picture.

Except for Margaret, Lisa was the first to awaken. She pulled herself up, resting against the back of the sofa, and sniffed the air. The pine tree scent and that of the fire had been joined by roasting turkey, and her mouth watered.

As if they were all awakened by it, like the Pied Piper's music, the other three raised their heads.

"Mmm, is that turkey?" Erin muttered, rubbing sleep from her eyes.

"Turkey and sunshine," Lisa said, waiting for Erin to realize the storm had ended.

"What? Oh, look!" she squeaked, throwing back the covers to rush over to the window. When she turned back to the others, her smile was radiant. "The storm's over!"

"We noticed," Ryan said, smiling at her enthusiasm, as he rested his head on one hand.

Paul, up on one elbow, stared at her but said nothing, his face solemn.

"Aren't you pleased, Paul?" she demanded. "The storm was so depressing! Just look how happy the world looks now that the sun is shining." Erin took several turns around the room, her exuberance translating itself into dance.

He grumbled under his breath and looked away.

"Want me to bring a cup of coffee to everyone?" Lisa offered. She thought that might be the best thing to avoid an argument. Caffeine might soothe Paul's irritation before Erin's enthusiasm disappeared.

Ryan shifted up against the back of the sofa and put his hands behind his head. "I like that idea. I always wanted you to serve me in bed."

They'd done a lot of things in bed, Lisa remembered, her cheeks flaming, but eating wasn't one of them. She ignored him. "I'll be back in a minute."

In the kitchen, her mother had the oven open and was basting the huge turkey, which probably explained why the aroma had awakened them suddenly.

"That smells delicious, but you're cooking a huge bird. We won't finish eating it until July," Lisa protested after greeting her mother.

"You'll be surprised how quickly it goes. Besides, there are lots of wonderful leftover turkey recipes," Margaret said.

"What we need right now is coffee to wake everyone up. I'm going to fix a tray and take it into the den."

"I had to get up at six o'clock to put the turkey on, so I baked homemade cinnamon rolls for breakfast. You can add them to the tray and everyone can eat in the den. That will keep the kitchen clear for me." Margaret hummed as she finished with the turkey, shoving the heavy bird back into the oven.

Lisa grinned. Her mother was in her element and didn't like to be disturbed. "Great. They'll love your cinnamon rolls." She added orange juice to the plate of rolls sitting out on the cabinet and then poured the boiling water into the cups of instant coffee. When she lifted the heavy tray, her mother gave her an absent wave of her hand, already involved in her next project.

"Great news!" Lisa called as she entered the den. "Homemade cinnamon rolls to go with the coffee."

Ryan got up and cleared everything off the square coffee table. "When did Margaret have time to make those?"

"She got up at six o'clock to put in the turkey."

Erin shivered. "I'm not sure I'd be that sacrificial. I hate getting up early."

Paul growled and Lisa hurriedly handed him a cup of coffee and a saucer with a roll on it.

Erin watched her before smiling at him. "Yes, Paul," she added as he started to refuse the roll, "eat the cinnamon roll. You could use a little sugar this morning."

"We don't all wake up cheerful, Erin," Ryan chided her. "Besides, I'd hate for these rolls to be wasted on someone who didn't appreciate them." He grinned at Lisa as he reached for another one.

"I don't think we have to worry about that with you, do we? Mom will be pleased." She turned to Erin. "She doesn't consider it a chore to get up early to cook. She really enjoys it."

"I suppose I'd do it, too, for a special occasion like Christmas dinner," Erin admitted grudgingly. She took a sip of her coffee and then set it down hurriedly. "Look! There are presents under the tree!"

Lisa shrugged her shoulders as Paul and Erin turned to look at her. "Mom just wanted to thank all of you for— for making this a better Christmas than last year."

"But we don't have anything for her," Erin wailed.

"She doesn't expect anything. You've given her a great deal," Lisa explained.

"Actually, I have a present for Frank and Margaret in the car. I think Margaret will still like it," Ryan murmured, avoiding Lisa's eyes.

She couldn't help but wonder if he'd brought a present for her, too. Not that she wanted a present from him, of course, but it was an intriguing idea.

Erin abandoned her breakfast to get down on her hands and knees and read the name tags on the three presents under the tree. "Oh, this one's mine," she said, picking up the package wrapped in green and red Santa paper.

"You're acting like a kid," Paul grumbled.

"I love presents," she said, shaking the box. "I wonder what it could be."

"It's not much, just a token of appreciation," Lisa warned, not sure what Erin would expect.

She grinned up at Lisa. "It doesn't really matter what it is. It's the thoughtfulness and the surprise. And trying to guess what it could be. We play guessing games at home for days before we unwrap the presents."

Lisa grinned in return. "I know. One year, Dad agreed with me when I told him what my presents were. I was depressed for several days until I figured out one of them couldn't possibly be what I thought. So I guessed again, and he agreed again. I cheered up right away when I realized I didn't really know what was in the boxes."

Ryan reached for another roll. "These cinnamon rolls are a better present than anything wrapped up under the tree. It's a good thing Margaret lives here and not in Dallas, or I'd gain a lot of weight."

"You need some kids to chase around the house," Erin teased, laughing at her friend. "That's how Mom and Dad stay slim."

"How many brothers and sisters do you have?" Lisa quickly asked, trying to dispel the immediate image of Ryan with children.

"Two sisters and two brothers," Erin said cheerfully. "I'm the oldest, and the youngest is seven." She leaned forward to say confidentially, "He was a surprise."

"How nice to have a big family," Lisa said with a sigh. "Mom and Dad were terrific, but sometimes it got lonely being an only child."

"I know," Ryan agreed. "I spent a lot of my childhood next door with the Stewards. Erin's mother took pity on me and let me share in their family life."

Lisa thought about Ryan's mother and realized just how lonely he must've been. At least she'd had wonderful parents. "I always said I'd have a huge family when I grew up just so my children wouldn't be alone," she said, a wistful smile on her face.

"Me, too," Ryan murmured, looking into her eyes.

She couldn't look away, seeing there unanswered questions, hopes, dreams that she had once shared. The thought of cradling Ryan's child against her breast was so beautiful it almost hurt. Finally, she wrenched her gaze from his.

"Anyone want another roll?" she asked, looking at the other two.

"Maybe I'd better have another one," Paul said. "I don't guess we'll eat Christmas dinner for a few hours."

"Mom likes to serve it about two o'clock. Then, for dinner, we just have leftovers. Sometimes, that's my favorite part."

"Have you ever sneaked downstairs and had pie for breakfast?" Erin asked, a guilty smile on her face.

Lisa nodded, "Yeah. Mom's coconut pie is incredible first thing in the morning."

"That sounds decadent," Ryan said.

"Indecent, I think," Paul agreed, but for the first time that morning he had a smile on his face.

"Is your mom making coconut pie this year?" Ryan asked.

"I hope so, or maybe chocolate, or—"

"Stop!" Ryan protested. "I'm stuffed with cinnamon rolls and you're making me hungry for pie. I'd better do some chores before I burst."

Lisa smiled. "You see, there's method in my madness. Now that the storm has ended, there are lots of chores. I'm planning on working you hard before Christmas dinner, because afterward you won't want to do anything but put your feet up by the fire."

"What kind of chores?" Paul asked warily.

"We'll have to clean off the driveway, the path to the barn, replenish—"

"Shovel the entire long drive?" Paul demanded, his expression incredulous. "We'll both have heart attacks."

Laughing, Lisa explained, "There's a mini-tractor with a snow plow attachment. We'll have to shovel the path to the barn and from around the cars, but the tractor does most of the work."

"That's a relief," Ryan muttered. "I was afraid I'd have to arm wrestle Paul for that last cinnamon roll to keep my strength up."

Everyone hooted at his words, offering various comments about the number he'd already eaten.

"Well, I can tell I won't get any sympathy here," he said, standing up. "I'm going upstairs and put on more clothes for our trek to the barn, partner," he said to Lisa. "Remember, we have to do the barn duties this morning since we lost last night."

"I'll go, Lisa. You stay here and help your mother," Paul said, standing.

"You didn't let us do the dishes last night, Paul," she reminded him. "I can't let you take my place this morning."

"But—"

"Everything will be fine. Hurry up, Ryan. I'm next." Lisa kept a smile in place until the door closed behind Ryan. "Really, Paul, we'll do just fine. And it's not as if you and Erin will get out of chores. I'll take the tray back to the kitchen and you two can strip the beds and turn them back into sofas. Then we'll need more wood brought in."

Paul reluctantly agreed. Erin immediately stood and started pulling the sheets from the beds and folding the quilts. Leaving them occupied, Lisa carried the tray to the kitchen.

"Your cinnamon rolls were a big hit, Mom, especially with Ryan," she said as she set down the tray and began unloading it.

"I do enjoy cooking for that boy. He has such a good appetite." She was beating something in a saucepan over a low heat.

"Mom, is that coconut pie you're making?"

"Of course, dear. That's your favorite, isn't it?"

"Yes, and if they stay another night, I'm going to do some serious hiding of what's left of it after dinner."

"What are you talking about?" Margaret asked, turning to look at her with a puzzled frown.

Lisa grinned. Ryan would've understood immediately, she thought. "Never mind. I'll explain later. Ryan and I are getting ready to go to the barn, and the others are tidying up the den. Then we're going to work on clearing the drive. Okay?"

"That will be lovely, dear. I'll just keep on working here." Margaret's thoughts had already turned back to her cooking.

Lisa waited until Ryan entered the kitchen to go upstairs. She didn't want any more rendezvous on the stairway. They were too much of a strain on her control. "I'll be down in a minute."

"No hurry," he assured her. "I'll probably find something to nibble on in here."

Margaret immediately turned around. "Didn't you have enough breakfast? I can make you some scrambled eggs if you want."

"Mom, don't listen to him. He was a pig about the cinnamon rolls," Lisa protested just as Erin came into the kitchen.

"That's better than being a pig about nothing at all," she grumbled.

"What are you talking about?" Lisa said.

"Paul. All he did was complain about how I folded the covers or refuse to speak to me at all. He doesn't have any Christmas spirit!"

"Maybe he's not a morning person," Ryan suggested. His gaze traveled on to Lisa as he said, "Too bad. Sometimes it's my favorite part of the day."

Lisa muttered, "I'll go get ready," and rushed out of the kitchen. She knew he was referring to their early-morning lovemaking. That had been her favorite part of the day also, when the realities of their life together hadn't yet intruded. Just the two of them, alone in their own little world.

But you had to get out of bed sometime.

SIXTEEN

"I'll go help you and Lisa in the barn," Erin suggested after Lisa left.

Ryan shook his head. "Nope. You stay here. Lisa and I will take care of the animals."

"But I enjoy— Oh, all right," she said, when Ryan fixed her with a hard stare. "But it's not fair."

Margaret chuckled. "That's a line children learn by heart by the time they're two. My students have to contribute a dime every time they say it. Then at the end of the year, we have a party with the money."

Grinning, Ryan said, "I'll bet you have some great parties."

"Yes, and we give part of the money to a charity to help people who really have a hard time."

"All right, I won't complain anymore," Erin said with a grimace. "But I do get to go outside when we're clearing the drive, don't I?"

"Of course. I'm sure there will be a snow shovel with your name on it," Ryan said.

Lisa came back into the kitchen, bundled up. "Ready?" she asked, avoiding Ryan's eyes.

"Yeah. We'll see you two in a little while," he added as he followed Lisa into the utility room.

There was a world of difference in their trip to the barn this morning. While it was still cold and the snow was deep, the sun shone brightly, reflecting off the whiteness. They pushed their way toward the barn, previously invisible.

Inside, Ryan put out an arm to stop Lisa as she moved toward Betsy. He shook his head when she drew back, a fearful look on her face.

"Stop it, Lisa. I'm not attacking you. I just wondered if I could try my hand at milking Betsy."

His request surprised a laugh from her. "Are you sure? She may be cranky this morning since she's been sick."

"I'd like to give it a shot. It's good to learn new things." He reached out his hand for the pail.

"Why don't we feed the chickens and gather eggs first and then I can, uh, supervise while you milk," she suggested, a smile on her face.

At least she wasn't treating him like the enemy, at least for a while, he thought. He nodded his head in agreement. Filling the bucket with the chicken feed, he enticed the hens from their nests.

Lisa gathered five eggs and Ryan four. "Shall we put them on the ground over by the door? Then we'll get them when we leave," Lisa said. "We don't want to break any more eggs or Mom will give up on us."

"A good idea," Ryan agreed. "I'm afraid I'll crush them as I bend over to milk if they go in my pockets now."

They took some straw and made a small nestlike resting place for the eggs by the door. Then, Lisa solemnly handed Ryan the pail.

"No instructions?"

"Well, all you do is squeeze gently with a sort of downward stroke." She laughed before adding, "You'll know you're doing it wrong if nothing comes out or Betsy kicks you.''

"Thanks a lot!"

"You can always change your mind," she offered.

"No. I'm determined."

He took the stool from the wall and set it down beside Betsy, taking a seat and placing the pail beneath her. "Okay, Betsy, old girl, here we go."

Lisa watched in silence as the first streams of milk went into the pail and Ryan smiled up at her. Then she said, "You're doing this because Paul knew how to milk and you didn't, aren't you?"

"What makes you think that?"

"Because it's like you said. You're determined. You go after what you want and you don't give up. I guess that's why you're so successful."

Ryan looked at her from the corner of his eye as he continued to milk. "Aren't you the same way? I'll bet you don't give up on a kid, even if he gives up on himself."

Betsy mooed, and Ryan gentled his milking style. He'd gotten a little intense with their conversation. When Lisa remained silent, he prompted, "Well?"

"I suppose not. But you make a lot of money."

"The world's values aren't always right. I can't do much to change that." He stopped milking and looked up at her. "I work hard, I share my wealth with others, and I try to do the right thing. I'm fortunate, I won't deny that. But I don't feel guilty."

"I'm not trying to make you feel guilty."

He returned to his milking.

"What do you mean, you share with others?" she asked.

"I give to charities, of course, those that I think are worthwhile, like the Women's shelter Erin works at. And I'm in the Big Brothers, Big Sisters program."

"You are?"

"Yeah, I've got a little brother. His name is Jeremy and he's something else."

"How do you have time for him?"

He could read her thoughts. He hadn't had time for her those few short weeks they were married. Looking up at her, he said deliberately, "I learned my lesson, Lisa. I don't ignore the people around me."

"What do you do with Jeremy? Buy him things?"

Her words angered him, but he forced himself to answer calmly. "Occasionally. But if he needs something, I usually give the money to his mom. She's a single parent and trying hard to make ends meet. I don't want Jeremy to see me as just a Santa Claus." He sighed. "Look, buying him something isn't the answer to Jeremy's problems. His father abandoned him and his mother three years ago. He's still hurting. We play basketball, hang out at McDonald's, go to a movie occasionally."

Lisa reached out and touched his hair, sending tremors through his body. "That's wonderful, Ryan," she whispered.

He reached up and caught her hand. "Don't give me more credit than you should. I enjoy spending time with Jeremy," he assured her, his voice hard. It irritated him that she would reach out to him for Jeremy's sake and yet not for himself.

"But—"

The barn door opened, halting her words, and they both remembered the eggs. Like a Greek chorus, they called out together, "Watch out for—"

Paul, coming in from the brilliant sunshine to the shadowy barn, put a booted foot smack in the middle of the little nest they'd made. The slimy results upended him at once.

They both hurried over to see if Paul was hurt. Betsy, disturbed by their action, shifted her position, kicking over the pail half full of milk.

Caught between the two disasters, Ryan and Lisa looked

at each other. Lisa's lips began to twitch and Ryan couldn't hold back the laughter that bubbled up in him.

"Damn! Margaret is never going to trust me in the barn again," he muttered, chuckling.

Lisa's laughter met his. "Nope. Never."

"Hey, I could've been hurt!" Paul called, outraged by their laughter. "Who was dumb enough to put the eggs here?" he demanded.

"Me," Lisa said. "I was supervising Ryan's milking."

"We didn't exactly expect callers," Ryan added apologetically. He reached out a hand to pull Paul to his feet. The man took it grudgingly, a frown still on his face. "What are you doing out here, anyway? Did the women chase you out of the house?"

"No. I came to get the snow shovels. Erin's dying to get outside, so I thought we'd start clearing out around the cars." He looked at Lisa. "Your mother said they were out here somewhere."

"They're in the storage room," Lisa said. As he turned to go get them, she added, "But I think you'll need to change your clothes. You've got egg yolk all over your jeans."

Ryan turned back to his own mess, hoping to hide his laughter from Paul. "That was a nasty thing to do, Betsy," he assured the cow, setting the pail upright.

Paul ignored Lisa and got the shovels from the storage room. "I'll take these back to the house and then change clothes. Are you two finished here?"

Looking at Lisa, Ryan asked, "Are we? Do I try to milk her anymore?"

"No. I think you'd just about finished." She grinned. "Both of you will have to confess to Mom what happened."

"Wait a minute," Ryan protested. "It's Paul's fault for falling. I was only trying to help him."

"And it's Lisa's fault I fell. After all, she's the one who put the eggs there. She's already said so," Paul added.

Lisa rolled her eyes. "Some gentlemen you are!" she teased. "I guess we'll all have to confess together. Come on. Let's go face Mom."

Margaret was philosophical about her losses and shrugged good-naturedly when the three explained the chaos in the barn.

"Don't worry about it. We have plenty of eggs, and I'm not sure Betsy's milk would've been drinkable anyway."

Paul edged toward the door. "I have to go change before I sit on anything. I've got egg all over my backside."

No one said anything until after he went through the door, but then Lisa and Ryan laughed again. "I know we shouldn't," she said to the other two women, "but everything happened so quickly. It was funny."

Margaret smiled, but Erin continued to frown.

"I think he got what he deserved," she said.

"He said he came to the barn to get the snow shovels because you wanted to go outside and work. Doesn't that count for something?" Ryan asked.

"He went to the barn to get away from me. I could've gotten the snow shovels. Where are they anyway?"

"In the utility room," Lisa said.

When Erin headed out the door, Margaret halted her. "Erin, I don't think you should go out alone. Wait until the others have a chance to warm up first. You might even make them a cup of coffee."

Though she was reluctant in her capitulation, Erin changed direction and went to the sink to fill the kettle. Lisa and Ryan shrugged out of their coats and sat down at the table.

"Have you called the airlines yet to see if there's a flight out this evening?" Ryan asked.

Erin's face brightened. "No, I forgot to do that. May I use the phone, Margaret?"

"Of course, child. If you use the one in the den, you'll be able to hear without us disturbing you."

Rushing toward the door, Erin suddenly halted. "Oh, the coffee."

"Don't worry about it. I can fix it when the water boils," Lisa assured her, sending her on her way.

"She's certainly anxious to join her family," Margaret commented, sitting down at the table with them.

"Or anxious to get away from Paul," Lisa added.

"They do seem to be getting on each other's nerves," Margaret agreed. "Which is odd because they got along so well when you first arrived."

Ryan nodded but said nothing. Lisa remembered his comment in the kitchen the evening before about Paul's frustration.

"Do you think it will affect our little company?" Margaret asked.

"No, I don't think so," Ryan finally said. "They won't have to live together, just work together. I think that will be easier."

"They won't even work together that much, Mom. Paul will be at school most of the day." The kettle whistled, reminding Lisa about the coffee. She got up and filled two mugs. "You want a cup?" she asked her mother.

"Yes, I believe I do."

"How's the dinner coming along?" Ryan asked.

"Just fine. But we won't eat for several more hours. Are you hungry?" Margaret responded to appetites like a calvary man to a bugle charge. "I can fix some sausage and cheese biscuits in no time."

"No, Mom, sit down and drink your coffee," Lisa said, but Ryan kept silent.

"You are hungry, aren't you?" Margaret demanded, a pleased smile on her face. "I'll have them ready in no time. You just take your coffee to the den, and I'll bring them in when they're ready."

"Thanks, Margaret," Ryan said, standing. He dropped a kiss on her cheek, grabbed his mug in one hand and Lisa's arm in the other, and headed for the den.

"You shouldn't have given Mom more work to do," Lisa protested as she was dragged along.

"She was beginning to worry about everything. I just distracted her," he explained, a superior look on his face.

"Are you sure that's what you were doing, and not just cadging another meal from her?"

He pushed her ahead of him into the den. "I won't turn down some more food. If we're going to shovel snow, we'll need it."

Erin was just hanging up the telephone. "I got us two seats on the seven o'clock flight to Denver. Do you think the roads will be open in time?"

"I'll call the sheriff's office and see," Lisa said, moving to the telephone. A couple of minutes later, she was able to reassure Erin. "They think they'll have them open by five. If you were going on to Colorado by road, you'd have more difficulties, but the storm didn't go too far south from here. It won't take as long to clear those roads."

The look on Erin's face was a mixture of relief and unhappiness. "If you don't mind, I'll call my parents and tell them when to expect us."

Lisa gestured to the phone, smiling, and walked over to the fireplace, warming her hands.

Ryan came over and stood beside her, staring down at the fire, but neither of them spoke. Behind them, they could hear Erin talking to her parents.

She hung up the phone and joined them. "Mother and Daddy are happy we'll finally arrive," she told Ryan.

"Good. How's the skiing?"

"Great. They haven't had any bad weather."

"At least you'll be able to get in a couple of days of skiing before you have to go back home," Lisa said, attempting to console her since she seemed so despondent. "I envy you. I haven't been in a couple of years."

"Come go with us," Ryan said.

Lisa turned her head sharply to stare at him before looking away. "No, I can't."

The door opened and Margaret entered, followed by Paul carrying a large tray.

"Paul arrived just in time to carry the tray for me," Margaret explained with a beaming smile. "This should keep you going until Christmas dinner."

After everyone thanked her, she hurried back to the kitchen as Paul moved to set the tray down on the coffee table.

"Seems someone needed a snack to keep going," he said, smiling at the others.

Erin, however, didn't show any appreciation for his smile. "That wouldn't be you, would it, Paul? You don't need anything . . . or anyone!" She strode over to the window, crossing her arms and staring outside.

"Brrr," Ryan muttered, "I think the temperature just dropped in here by about fifty degrees. What did you say to her while we were out at the barn?"

Paul dug his fists into his pockets and stared across the room at Erin as he spoke. "Nothing that terrible. She just wanted to make plans for—for all of us getting together when we got back to Dallas. I guess I was a little evasive."

"We should eat Mom's snack before it gets cold. I'll get Erin. You two go ahead and eat," Lisa said as she walked across the room.

When she reached the window, she stood beside Erin quietly, trying not to notice the tear that was tracing its way down her cheek.

"How about a cup of coffee and a cheese and sausage biscuit?"

"Thanks, but I'm not hungry."

"Do you want Paul to think he's ruined your appetite? That would be like letting him think he'd won," Lisa whispered.

"Won what?" Erin asked, wiping her cheek with the back of her hand.

"Your heart." She smiled when Erin stared at her. "Come on. You don't have much longer. Try to pretend he's some stranger you know nothing about." She tugged on Erin's arm. "Besides, when we get outside in the snow, you'll be grateful for the extra calories."

When Erin still didn't budge, Lisa used her best argument. "And when we're outside, we'll plaster them with snowballs to get our revenge."

"What are they whispering about?" Paul asked, his eyes trained on the two women.

"I don't know, but I don't think it will be something we like. If they gang up on us, we'll be in trouble," Ryan said, taking a second biscuit.

"Lisa?" Paul called. "You two had better hurry or Ryan will eat everything."

"We're coming," she sang out cheerfully, pulling Erin toward the table. "I was just telling Erin how good these biscuits are. I guess Ryan can testify to that."

Erin said nothing, avoiding the men's eyes as she sat down beside Ryan. Lisa joined Paul on the other sofa and handed a cup of coffee to Erin.

"She's right, Erin. These are terrific," Ryan assured her.

"You may have to do all the shoveling by yourself if you eat any more of those," Lisa teased, relieved that Ryan wasn't sulking or mad. It was hard enough dealing with the other two.

"Not me. I believe in women's liberation. I want to let you share in the joy of shoveling."

"Isn't that just like a man?" Erin said, speaking for the first time. "The only time they believe in women's liberation is when it will be to their advantage."

"We can certainly manage to do the job without your help if you feel you're not strong enough," Paul said stiffly, glaring at her.

"Oh, Paul, for heaven's sake," Lisa complained, "quit

being such a killjoy. If this is the way you've acted all morning, I don't blame Erin for losing her patience.''

"What did I tell you?" Ryan said. "Women always stick together. Pretty soon, they'll be accusing me of being a grouch just because you've been one this morning.''

"Just shut up and eat another biscuit," Paul growled.

"Gladly." Ryan seemed to take no offense and suited his action to his words.

Erin, however, was outraged. "How dare you speak to Ryan that way. He hasn't done anything wrong!''

"I didn't say he had," Paul returned.

"For that matter, neither have I," Erin continued, building steam. "But you've treated me like an outcast all morning.''

"You think you haven't done anything?" Paul demanded, his voice rising.

"Just what have I done? I've tried to be nice to you, that's all. Is that so terrible?''

Lisa sat there with her mouth open, appalled at the anger that had broken out. She looked over at Ryan, hoping for some assistance in stopping the full-blown argument, only to find him smiling, munching on a biscuit, as if nothing were happening.

"Erin, Paul," she began, "Why don't—"

"Well?" Erin demanded, ignoring Lisa. "Tell me, what have I done?''

Paul stood, his cheeks flushed, and demanded, "You want to know what you've done? You want to know what you've done?''

"Yes," Erin shouted, standing to face him nose to nose. "Tell me what I've done!''

"Nothing! That's what you've done. Except look so damn sexy you're driving me crazy!" Without waiting for a reply, he turned and stomped out of the room, slamming the door behind him.

The fire crackled merrily and Ryan took a sip of coffee,

but the two women stood staring after Paul as if turned to stone.

Lisa didn't know how long she'd stood, but a deep chuckle from Ryan brought her awake.

She looked at him, frowning. "What are you laughing about?"

Erin spun around to face him also, waiting for his reply.

He leaned forward and set his coffee cup down on the table. "I'm laughing because I know just how he feels." He stood and strolled to the door. As he opened it, he looked over his shoulder and winked. "See you outside, ladies."

SEVENTEEN

"I don't know whether to laugh or cry," Erin complained, looking at Lisa.

"I certainly couldn't tell you. I'm just as confused as you are."

Erin flopped down on the sofa. "But he hasn't even *tried* to do anything! If he's attracted to me, why hasn't he?"

Sighing, Lisa sat down also. "Maybe he thought you and Ryan—"

"How could he think that when Ryan can't take his eyes off you? It's obvious he doesn't care about me, at least not that way." Erin stood up and paced across the room. "Men! They are impossible to understand."

Margaret stuck her head in the door. "Is everything all right?"

Lisa stood up. "Yes, Mom. We're just gathering the dishes. We'll be in the kitchen in just a minute."

Margaret disappeared behind the door. Placing the mugs on the tray, Lisa picked it up. "What now? Do you want to stay here and let them do the work by themselves?"

Erin sprang up from her chair as if there'd been an electrical surge. "No way! I'm not going to let Paul think

I'm incapable of doing any work. I'm going out there and outshovel that he-man!'' She surged forward and out the door before Lisa could even blink.

Left standing alone in front of the fireplace, Lisa considered sitting back down and letting them fight it out alone. She was tired of the emotional stress of all this togetherness.

Shaking her head, she followed in Erin's footsteps. She couldn't do that. Besides, the togetherness wasn't bothering her. At least, most of the togetherness. It was Ryan who was causing all her stress. She was torn between the fairy tale love and the everyday reality.

''Erin just went outside,'' Margaret said as Lisa entered the kitchen. ''Are you sure everything's all right?''

''No, I'm not. She and Paul are at odds with each other. I'd better get outside and prevent a major war from breaking out.''

''You do remember how to operate the tractor, don't you?''

''Yes.'' Lisa donned her outer garments and walked out into the bright sunshine. It certainly felt better than the stiff winds that had blown the snow. But the temperature was still way below freezing. Ahead of her, Paul was furiously tossing snow aside on the path to the barn. She couldn't see Erin or Ryan.

Walking along the cleared path, she tapped him on the shoulder and then stepped back as he almost snarled at her.

''Whoa! I'm not the enemy, Paul.''

''Sorry, Lisa.''

''Do you need to take a breather? Shoveling snow can be pretty strenuous.''

''No. I need to work until I drop. Then maybe I won't have the energy to make a fool of myself.'' He turned away to start shoveling again.

Lisa started to reassure him but stopped herself. Words wouldn't make any difference to him at this point. She changed direction, stepping into the deep snow to cross the yard to the shed where her father always kept the tractor.

The snowplow was already in place. She checked the gas gauge and then pushed open the sliding doors. It took several tries to fire up the engine. Then she eased forward on the gas pedal as she lowered the snowplow. Thank goodness for man's inventions.

As she slowly rounded the house, she discovered Ryan and Erin by the garage. Ryan was using the second snow shovel to dig out the cars while Erin was using a broom to sweep the snow from the cars. Lisa waved as she started down the long driveway leading to the road.

Her breath hung in the air as the tractor chugged along. Piles of white snow fell to the side in front of the plow. She used to ride on her father's knees when he did this particular chore, enjoying being outside after a storm. He'd let her drive within the circle of his arms. Would she ever have a child to whom she could teach the small wonders of life? A child to protect and yet teach? A child to share the joys of love and life, of Christmas?

As she reached the end of the drive, she saw black smoke about a mile down the road. The highway people were already out clearing the roads. By the time she'd done the other side of the drive, it would be necessary to come back and shove aside the pile of snow the big machine would dump on their drive. She swung the tractor around and headed back toward the house.

Ryan stood by the cars watching her as she reached the garage again. She came to a halt and killed the motor and he moved over to stand beside her.

"That's a nice little machine."

"Yeah. It's a little bit faster than the shovel." She looked for Erin. "Where's Erin?"

"She went to check on Paul."

"Do you think that's a good idea?" Lisa stepped down from the tractor, intent on preventing more argument.

Ryan caught her arm. "Lisa, you can't hit their hands with a ruler. They're adults."

"I didn't intend to. Besides, that's not how a teacher treats her students these days." She pulled her arm away just as Erin rounded the house.

"Is Paul okay?" Lisa asked, watching the other's face.

"Fine. Just as friendly as ever. He's almost finished the path to the barn." Erin turned to stare down the driveway as the big snowplow came by.

"Does that mean the roads are open?" she demanded of Lisa.

"Well, he came from town and he'll keep going to the county line, and then he'll turn around and clear the other side. Once he's finished, the road will be clear to the county line. Whenever that county's snowplow gets there, then the road will be cleared."

Sighing with frustration, Erin muttered, "I wish we could just get in the car and leave at once."

"Mom's put a lot of work into Christmas dinner, Erin," Lisa said gently. "It means a lot to her."

"Oh, I know. I wouldn't do that to Margaret," Erin promised, touching Lisa's shoulder. "It's just that I get so frustrated with that man!"

"Why don't I go clear the end of the driveway, and you two can go inside and clean up for dinner," Ryan suggested.

"You know how to drive a tractor?"

"This one's easy. I drove a forklift one summer," he bragged, sliding onto the seat.

"Just don't go too fast," she warned, watching as he made a wide circle and headed back down the driveway.

"Don't worry about Ryan. He'll do whatever he sets out to do," Erin said. "Shall we go back in?"

"There's no hurry unless you're cold. We've got a couple of hours until dinner. Want to build a snowman?" Lisa suggested. Her father had always helped her, since she had no brothers or sisters, until she was old enough to have friends over to mold their cold companion.

"A snowman? Wow! I didn't even think of that. We don't get the opportunity often in Dallas."

The two of them began their sculpturing. At first they intended to build a modest snowman. Then, as their enthusiasm grew, so did their snowman. By the time Ryan returned with the tractor, the two of them had a huge mound of snow for the bottom of the snowman.

"What are you two doing?"

"What do you think? We're building a snowman!" Erin shrieked as she lost her footing and sat down hard in the snow.

"It's a good thing you didn't fall forward or you would've flattened it," he teased.

"Aren't you going to help us?" Lisa demanded, watching him as he sat on the tractor.

"I suppose so, or you won't get finished for dinner. Why did you have to build such a large one?"

"They're the best kind," Lisa assured him with a superior smile.

"Naturally. I'll put the tractor away and come back to help." He drove away from the two women, shaking his head but with a smile on his face. They were acting like children and enjoying every minute of it.

Someday he intended to have children and teach them how to enjoy things like snowmen, baseball, chocolate cake, the good things in life. He was learning a lot about childhood from Jeremy. Now he was ready to apply it to his own child.

"Hey, Paul!" he called as he neared the shed.

Paul was standing beside the barn, resting on the snow shovel, surveying the path he'd just cleared. He picked up the shovel and walked toward Ryan.

By the time Ryan had parked the tractor and was shoving the doors closed, Paul was there. "Yeah? The driveway clear?"

"Yep, all finished. And Erin cleared off the cars."

"Okay."

"The ladies have requested our assistance with another project, however," Ryan said smoothly, watching Paul closely.

"What now?"

"A snowman."

Paul's eyes widened and Ryan saw the first signs of enjoyment the man had shown in several days. Then he immediately clamped down and looked away. "I'm cold."

"Come on, Paul. We're going to leave this afternoon. You might as well get some enjoyment from our predicament. How often did you get to make a snowman in Cleburne?"

He turned and grinned at Ryan. "Never."

"Then don't pass up this opportunity." Ryan grabbed him by the arm and pulled him back toward the front of the house. "You won't believe the size of the snowman those two crazy women are making."

When they saw the mound of snow, Paul just stood and stared. "That's crazy!"

"That's what I said."

"Come on, guys, help us!" Lisa called out, waving to them.

Paul walked forward and stood staring at their efforts, his hands on his hips. "Don't you think you should be a little less ambitious?"

"Nope," Erin replied, not looking at him. "We've got big dreams, and we're going for it."

Ryan grinned and nudged Paul. "Dreams won't do it alone. It takes elbow grease. Let's get busy."

The rest of the morning was spent building their snowman. Lisa raided her mother's sewing box for large black buttons for his eyes and got a carrot for the nose and several strips of red licorice for the mouth. She found an old straw hat of her father's and placed it on top as the crowning touch.

"Isn't he wonderful?" Erin asked everyone, staring up at their creation.

"Yeah," Paul agreed, satisfaction in his voice.

Ryan turned to look for Lisa, tired but pleased, ready to share the moment with her. His timing was perfect. The snowball hit him square on his chest.

"Hey!" he yelled just as several more icy missiles were thrown at the three of them.

"What's going on?" Paul demanded.

"A snowball fight!" Lisa cried as she threw another.

Ryan ducked for cover at once, hiding behind their snowman. Erin, too, ran for cover behind one of the cars. Paul stood still, stupefied, until a snowball from Erin caught him on the shoulder. With a howl of revenge, he lunged for her hiding place.

Erin ran screaming to Lisa's side and the two ladies banded together to fend off the gentlemen approaching with a swiftly made arsenal of snowballs.

It wasn't long before they were routed and chased to the back door of the house. All four entered the utility room in a much better frame of mind than when they'd left it.

"Dinner is in an hour," Margaret said as they filed into the kitchen. "Enough time for a cup of coffee and getting out of your wet things."

"Erin, you take the bath first and I'll fix coffee. You guys make sure the fire's nice and hot," Lisa ordered, moving to the stove.

"Yes, ma'am," Ryan said, saluting her and leaving her kitchen with the other two.

"Did everything get worked out?" Margaret asked.

"I think so. We had a snowball fight."

"Ah, that would explain all the snow in your hair," Margaret said calmly.

"Ryan caught me." Lisa smiled as she remembered his bear hug that wrestled her down to the snow, followed by a stolen kiss before he dumped a handful of snow on her face.

"I heard the snowplow go by earlier."

"Yes. Ryan cleared off the end of the drive afterward," Lisa assured her mother. "They should be able to leave after dinner."

"And Paul?"

Lisa shook her head. "I don't know when he's going to leave. Are you in a hurry for him to go, too?"

"No, of course not. I've enjoyed having all of them here. It's been a wonderful Christmas for me, dear. I was just worried about you." Margaret didn't look up from the holly-green icing she was putting on a cake.

"Everything will be fine, Mom," she assured her, dropping a kiss on her cheek. "It's been a wonderful Christmas for me, too, in spite of how I thought it would be at first."

And it had. She still missed her father. But she understood what he'd been trying to tell her about her marriage. She'd run away.

She still didn't know if a marriage between the two of them would work, but she was willing to try. When she got back to Dallas, she intended to call Ryan and suggest . . . she didn't know what to suggest. She just knew she didn't want to lose him.

Everyone made a special effort to look nice for Margaret's Christmas dinner. The table was covered with a deep green tablecloth, and there was a red poinsettia centerpiece. Even though there was enough light from outside, Margaret lit two tall red candles on each side of the plant.

At one end of the table she had Ryan place the huge bronzed turkey, its steamy aroma making mouths water. At the other end, she had a sliced ham. In between were all the traditional dishes Lisa remembered—cranberry sauce, fruit salad mixed with whipped cream and pecans, pea salad, her mother's special dressing, homemade rolls, and macaroni and cheese.

On the kitchen counter were the coconut pie, chocolate pie, Christmas cake, and pecan pie. As a child, Lisa had always wanted to start with pie. Now she appreciated the other food, but she spared a lingering glance at the desserts, reminding herself to save room.

When they were all seated at the table, Margaret extended her hands to Lisa on her left and Ryan on her right. "If you don't mind, we always hold hands to say the blessing at Christmas dinner."

Lisa extended her hand to Paul and Ryan to Erin, but Paul and Erin hesitated before joining their hands for the final link.

After thanking God for the food and the blessings, Margaret paused and then said, "A special thanks for bringing these friends to our table, for easing the pain we suffered, for giving us the peace and the hope of Christmas." Her amen was echoed around the table.

There was a pleasant jumble of voices as the food was shared. Ryan carved the turkey and passed out slices of the tender, juicy meat. Their outside activities had enhanced their appetites, and they all enjoyed their meal.

When Margaret got up to serve the dessert, there were several denials until she brought the pies and cake over to the table. Then even Erin agreed to eat just one small piece of her favorite.

When everyone had finished, Margaret said, "I know you're anxious to get to the airport, Erin, Ryan, but there's just one more thing. I have a small gift for each of you." She held up her hand when they would've protested.

"I don't want to get too sentimental, but I was dreading this Christmas. You've all made it a wonderful experience, and you've given me things to look forward to. I just wanted to give you a little something to say thank you."

She went into the den and brought back the three presents.

Erin and Paul both expressed their appreciation for the gifts, with Erin saying the colors of the eyeshadows and lipsticks were perfect for her. When Ryan opened his, Margaret said, "I made that for Frank for last Christmas, Ryan. I hope you don't mind."

"No, Margaret, I'm honored that you've given it to me. I'll think of him every time I wear it."

She blinked back the moisture in her eyes. "Good. He really enjoyed—knowing you."

He leaned over and kissed her cheek. "I brought a gift for you and Frank, Margaret. I wasn't sure what to do about it, but after our conversation the other evening, I think you might enjoy it."

"What is it?" she asked, her eyes lighting up.

He stood and walked over to the cabinet where he'd put an envelope when he'd entered the kitchen. "Remember when we were talking about a cruise? Well, I ended up with a lot of stock in a cruise ship company in a deal I just finished, so I bought you and Frank a cruise. Would you like to take a friend with you?"

The large envelope had brochures showing the boat and the individual cabins. Margaret was excited as she showed it to Lisa.

Lisa tried to be happy for her mother, but it was obviously an expensive gift. She said nothing, however.

Margaret looked at Ryan and expressed the same thought. "Ryan, this is much too expensive."

"I got a special deal, Margaret. Besides, you deserve it." He smiled at both of them, and neither woman could resist the warmth there.

Trying to express her thanks to him without words, Lisa smiled and nodded her head. Now her mother had something else to look forward to.

"We'd better start doing the dishes if we're going to make our flight," Erin finally said. She avoided Paul's eyes as she stood and picked up several dishes.

"Here, now," Margaret protested. "I've got the rest of the day to clean up. I certainly won't be cooking for several days with all these leftovers. You just scoot upstairs and do your packing and leave all this to me.''

In spite of everyone's protests, Margaret shooed them all out of the kitchen, sending Lisa up to help Erin pack. The two women stood in Lisa's room, smiling at each other, before Lisa reached out to hug Erin.

''I didn't think I would like you, Erin, but I feel like I'm losing a friend.''

''Not losing me, Lisa. I'm just going away for a while. We'll get together as soon as we're both back in Dallas. In spite of what Paul thinks.'' There was an edge of bitterness to her voice that saddened Lisa.

''Don't be too hard on Paul. Schoolteachers aren't used to the beautiful life. It's frightening.''

''Is that what happened to you and Ryan?'' Erin asked as she pulled out her suitcase and opened it on the bed.

''Something like that.'' Lisa avoided her gaze.

''I wish you'd give him another chance.''

Lisa stood and walked over to the dresser, toying with a figurine she'd had since she was eight. ''I'd like to. I'm going to—to talk to him when we're all back in Dallas. I don't think we're ready to, uh, marry again, but we can get to know each other.''

Erin gave her another hug. ''Good. Now help me dump everything in here. It's getting late and I don't want to miss my plane. I've missed my family.''

Lisa emptied drawers with Erin. ''Yes. Christmas is a time for family. But thank you for sharing ours.''

It didn't take Ryan long to pack his one bag. But he wasn't ready to leave yet. When he'd arrived here, he only knew he had to see Lisa again. Now he realized that, for all his vaunted determination, he'd given up on the most important thing in the world to him, his marriage.

Perhaps it was fear of failure, something he'd never experienced before. Perhaps it was the appalling example of his parents' marriage. But he hadn't fought for his marriage.

In spite of all the reasons he had to leave, he didn't want to leave Lisa, to give up again. He didn't want to spend Christmas day away from her. In fact, the thought of leaving her sent an inexplicable panic through him, as if he'd never have another chance to reclaim his happiness.

He zipped his bag and stood staring at the wall.

"Ryan? You okay?" Paul asked.

"Yeah." He set the bag on the floor. "I'll be right back." Before Paul could say anything, he strode down the hall and pounded on Lisa's bedroom door. "Lisa?"

When she opened the door, he rapped out, "Pack a bag. You're coming with us!"

EIGHTEEN

"What?" Lisa questioned, staring at him.

"Pack your bags. You're coming with us," he repeated, his jaw squared and determination in his eyes.

"I'm doing no such thing," she returned.

"Lisa, listen to me. I let you run away last time. Now, I'm not quitting on us. We're staying together and working things out."

"Do I not have a choice in this?" she demanded, her voice rising. "Does the world have to march to your beat? Isn't this exactly what happened before? You did what you wanted and I was expected to fall in behind, no questions asked?"

"No! That's not what happened! Those were special circumstances. And you're the one who quit, who ran away."

By now both were yelling and they had an audience. Paul had come out of the bedroom he'd shared with Ryan, and Erin was standing behind Lisa in the bedroom.

"Maybe I did, but I had good reasons. And they haven't changed any as far as I can tell!"

"You really don't love me, do you?" He drew a deep breath and lowered his voice to a throaty growl. "Then there's nothing else to say." He stomped back to the other bedroom to retrieve his suitcase, and Lisa slammed the door, shutting him out.

"Lisa—" Erin began, but Lisa cut her off.

"Don't say anything. Just go so we can remain friends." Holding back the tears, she hugged Erin again and helped her set the suitcases in the hallway. Then, in spite of her mother's good training, she returned to her room and closed the door.

She heard footsteps in the hall and voices, followed a moment later by Margaret's voice calling a farewell and the front door closing. A car's engine started up and gradually faded away. He was gone.

Tears scalded her cheeks as she gradually gave in to the misery that filled her. He was gone.

After the storm of tears, she lay still, her mind beginning to function again. She realized she'd made a mistake. She'd wanted everything worked out before she committed herself to him again. She'd wanted a guarantee she wouldn't be hurt.

But life didn't come with a guarantee. And opportunity didn't knock every day. And in spite of knowing those clichés, she'd blown it.

Next time, she whispered to herself. Next time, if there was a next time, she'd put her heart on the line and take a chance on happiness. She closed her eyes and prayed for a next time.

A knock on her door made her eyes pop open. Had he returned? Was this her next time? She rushed to the door to find Paul waiting. Trying to hide her abject disappointment, she gave a wobbly smile.

"Lisa, I'm going to leave now."

"Now? But you won't get home until late."

"I know, but—but I don't mind driving at night."

She read the misery to match her own in his eyes. "I'm sorry things didn't work out. I didn't intend—"

"No, neither did I. Let me know when your flight gets into Dallas and I'll pick you up at the airport."

"All right, thanks. Paul," she added as he was turning away, "don't make the same mistake as me."

"No, I won't," he promised, his voice hard.

"You don't understand. My mistake wasn't marrying Ryan." She gulped, forcing herself to continue. "My mistake was leaving him, letting things affect our marriage." She reached out and touched his arm. "Love is hard to come by. Don't throw it away for pride."

Her words didn't make him happy. He reached out for her and held her in his arms briefly. "I don't know what to do."

"I know."

He released her and stepped back. "I'll see you back in Dallas."

"In spite of my earlier poor manners, I'll see you to the door," she assured him.

They stopped in the kitchen for him to tell Margaret good-bye. She insisted on making him several sandwiches to take with him. When a tin of cookies had been added to his belongings, along with the sandwiches, Margaret wished him good-bye.

At the door, Lisa hugged him again. "Be careful," she said, trying to smile.

"I will. Take care." He strode to his car, waved once after he'd stored his belongings in the backseat, and then drove down the long driveway and headed south toward Amarillo.

Margaret came into the den when she heard the front door close. "How strange to be just the two of us."

"Yes."

"Are you all right?" she asked, coming to Lisa's side and putting an arm around her.

"I suppose for an idiot I'm okay."

"Now, dear, you aren't an idiot. A little stubborn sometimes, perhaps."

Lisa sighed. "More than a little."

"Things will work out. You'll see." Margaret hugged her close and then released her. "I still have some cleaning up to do in the kitchen."

"I'll come help you. Maybe it will keep me from thinking."

With both of them working, they were finished in half an hour. Margaret took off her apron and hung it up.

"If you don't mind, Lisa, I'm going to deliver some of these tins of cookies and see how my neighbors weathered the storm. Would you like to come with me?"

"No thanks, Mom, but you go ahead. Just be careful out on the road."

"I'm an old hand at driving in this mess, child, as well you know. I'll be back in an hour or two." She gathered up the cookie tins and loaded them in a shopping bag. Putting on her coat, she headed outdoors.

Lisa looked around the empty kitchen. She couldn't see anything else to be done. With a sigh, she wandered back into the den and put another log on the fire. Settling down on the sofa, she stared up at the Christmas tree.

The firelight was reflected in the icicles and some of the ornaments, giving it a lively glow. They'd done a good job of decorating, except for the bare spot on top. Why couldn't she remember what they'd done with the star?

Why couldn't she get her life straightened out, too? Tears gathered in her eyes, but she sniffed, trying to hold them back. There was no point in feeling sorry for herself. Her father had always taught her to fight for what she wanted. She hadn't done that.

And that's why her life was as barren as the top of the Christmas tree.

She closed her eyes, overwhelmed with misery. The distant sound of a car didn't penetrate her thoughts until it grew much closer. Frowning, she wondered why her mother was returning so quickly. She couldn't possibly have visited all those on her list.

Lisa wiped her wet cheeks and stiffened her shoulders. She didn't want to make her mother miserable as well as herself.

A knock on the front door surprised her. If the car hadn't been her mother's, it must be a neighbor, doing the same thing as her mother. She walked over and swung open the door.

"Aren't you going a little fast?" Erin finally asked.

"Why do you say that?" Ryan snapped. He automatically looked at the speedometer and muttered under his breath. He also let up on the gas pedal. "Sorry."

"Ryan, I don't think—"

"Erin, stay out of this."

She leaned back against the upholstery and said nothing else for several miles. "I'm going to say it anyway. I think you overreacted!" she burst out.

He tightened his lips and clutched the steering wheel in a death grip.

Several more miles passed. "Aren't you going to say *anything*?" she asked.

He glared at her, wishing she would leave him alone. He didn't want to think about what had just happened. He knew he'd overreacted. Panicked might be a better word. Letting Lisa leave had been pure hell. Somehow, leaving without her now had felt the same. So he'd tried to strong-arm her. He should've known it wouldn't work.

"You don't have to go to Colorado with me."

"What?" he snapped, staring at her again.

"I'm a big girl, Ryan. You don't have to escort me to Colorado. Just drop me off at the airport and go back to Lisa."

He thought about what she'd said. Would Lisa even let him in the door? Margaret would. He could try to talk to

Lisa, to explain his feelings, his panic. Would she listen? Eventually.

"Are you sure you don't mind?"

"No, of course not. You and Lisa are right for each other." She grinned. "But I'm not going to be the one to break the news to your mother."

"No. I'll do that. Along with a few home truths," he said grimly. "I may have made some mistakes, but she added to them."

Now that the decision was made, he relaxed a little. He wasn't giving up. He and Lisa might have another chance. Erin, too, seemed more at ease. Or maybe that was because he wasn't trying to break speed records.

A few minutes later, she gasped.

"What is it?" he demanded, sparing her a look.

"That looks like Paul's car behind us."

"Wasn't he staying until tomorrow, at least?" Ryan asked, trying to see in his rearview mirror.

"I don't know. He wasn't exactly chatty with me the last day or two," she said miserably.

"Do you think it's him?"

"It looks like his car."

Ryan began slowing down.

"What are you doing?"

"Stopping. If that's Paul, he'll stop, too."

"But why?" Erin demanded, her voice tensing.

"If he's going to Amarillo, I can get him to drop you off at the airport, if you don't mind, and let me get back to Lisa." He kept his eyes on the car behind him.

"I don't think he'll want to do that."

Ryan said nothing, pulling the car to a stop beside the road. The other car pulled in behind him. "Wait here."

He jumped out of his car and ran to the passenger side of the other vehicle. Opening the door, he slid into the seat. "I didn't know you were leaving so soon," he said, looking at Paul.

"It seemed like the thing to do."

"I need to ask a favor."

Surprised, Paul nevertheless said, "Sure."

"Would you take Erin to the airport for me? I've decided to go back and camp on Lisa's doorstep until she agrees to at least see me again."

Paul stared at him, finally smiling. "Sure. You and Lisa deserve to be happy. I'll take care of Erin for you."

"Thanks, pal. I'll see you in Dallas. And I owe you a big one."

"Remind me to collect," Paul agreed, laughing.

Ryan returned to his car.

"It's a deal. Paul's going to take you to the airport. And if you can't get him to use the extra ticket to Denver, my treat, you're not worth a plug nickel," he teased.

Erin's eyes lit up. "Do you think— No, he'd never agree."

Ryan shrugged. "He's doing me a favor. Tell him it's partial payment. Come on, I'll get your bags."

Once the transfer was made, Ryan waved the other two good-bye and swung his car around to head west back to Dalhart.

"May I come in?" Ryan asked.

Lisa moved back, silently gesturing for him to enter, wondering all the while if this was her second chance. "Did you forget something?"

"Yes."

He walked over to stand by the fire, extending his hands to the blaze. After a moment of silence, he turned to face her. "Yes, I forgot something."

"What?" she whispered.

"You."

Her heart contracted with painful hope. Was there still a chance for their marriage? Did he still love her? "You came back for me?"

"Yes, only this time, I'm not ordering you to come with me. I'm going to stay with you until you give in."

When she would've responded, he held up a hand, advancing toward her as he said, "I know we have a lot of things to work out, Lisa, but I promise we will work them out. I didn't put you first last time, but I've learned that lesson. My mother wasn't exactly welcoming, and it was a mistake for us to live with her, even for a few weeks. That's changed."

"I know."

"I didn't understand what teaching meant to you before, but I won't object to your teaching. When we start a family, we'll discuss it again, but I want you to be happy."

"I know."

"I can't promise everything will always go smoothly, but I can promise that I won't let go, that I won't give up. We'll deal with the money issue, and any other issue that comes up, together. We'll work things out, if you'll just give me a chance," he promised, grasping her shoulders and staring intently at her.

"I know."

"What do you mean?" he demanded, shaking her. "Tell me what you're thinking."

Lisa smiled up at him, her heart in her eyes. "I know all those things. I knew them when you knocked on my door a couple of hours ago. But I panicked because I was afraid of being hurt again. I love you, Ryan, just as I always have, ever since I first saw you."

His lips covered hers as he swept her up into his arms, and skyrockets burst in Lisa's mind as she finally returned to the place she belonged. He raised his head long enough for her to say, "Thank you for coming back, for giving me another chance."

His only response was another embrace that escalated rapidly. Pressed tightly against him, Lisa was as aware of his arousal as she was of her own, but this time, she had no qualms about surrendering to him. He was her husband in her heart, even if he wasn't legally.

Ryan drew back. "We'd better stop this or your mother might be embarrassed to walk in and find us on the sofa making love."

Lisa linked her hands behind his neck and reached up to caress his strong jaw. "Mom's not here," she whispered suggestively.

Ryan actually took a step back from her, pulling away from her arms.

"What's wrong?" she asked, watching him fearfully.

"Nothing, but I promised myself I wouldn't make love to you until we were together again. I don't know if I can keep that promise if I keep holding you, knowing that we're alone."

Lisa smiled dreamily at the worried frown on Ryan's brow and moved a step closer to reach up and smooth it away. "I certainly hope you can't," she murmured before her lips met his.

"Lisa!" he protested, only after having cooperated fully with her kiss. "I'm serious."

"Ryan," Lisa said solemnly, wrapping her arms around his middle, "you promised me you'd never leave me, and I offer you the same promise. I'll stay and fight it out, whatever the problem. I won't run away again."

He dropped a quick kiss on her lips. "Good. Can we go to Vegas and get married at once so I don't have to wear out my self-discipline?"

"I have a better idea. I think we should wait a couple of days and get married here."

He groaned, rubbing his hands over her back, his lips nibbling at her neck. "I don't think I can wait that long."

"I don't think you can either," Lisa agreed, pressing her hips against his with a seductive chuckle. "And I don't want you to. I know a perfectly good bed upstairs, just waiting for us."

"Are you sure?" he asked, staring down at her. "I don't want to rush you into anything."

She buried her face in his chest. "I've been aching for

you for the past year and a half. Don't make me beg,''
she pleaded, raising her face to look at him.

Without another word, he swung her up into his arms
and headed for the second floor. Lisa looked over his
shoulder at the Christmas tree, at the vacant place at its
top. At least something was right this Christmas. She was
being given a new start, a chance for happiness.

NINETEEN

Lisa lay wrapped in Ryan's arms, sated with the most glorious lovemaking she'd ever experienced. Their greater knowledge of each other, as well as the depth of their love, made the past few moments all the more life-shattering.

"Ryan?"

"Hmmm?"

"I love you."

"I love you, sweetheart. And I've missed you."

"Me, too."

Snuggled under the covers, Lisa thought she'd never move from Ryan's side again. She remembered her father's encouragement to a least talk with Ryan, to make an effort to work things out. He was right. She'd run away.

Now she was back home again. She only hoped her father knew.

"Lisa?"

"Mmmm?"

"When is your mother coming back home?"

"I don't know. Any time now."

"Shouldn't we get dressed? I don't want to shock her."

"I may never get dressed again," she said, snuggling against his warmth, stroking his chest, letting her fingers slide through the silky hairs.

"Sounds good to me. But teaching might be kind of difficult," he teased, kissing her neck.

Lisa giggled, feeling lighthearted and lazy. She looked over Ryan's shoulder, scarcely focusing on anything until she noted through the open door of her closet a red box on the shelf. She jerked away from Ryan as if he'd bitten her.

"Lisa?" he questioned in surprise as she threw back the covers and dashed to the closet. "What are you doing?"

"The star! There's the star!"

"I don't see—"

"In the box," she exclaimed as she reached up for it, providing him an excellent view of all her charms.

"What's it doing there?"

"Last Christmas I wanted—I just wanted to cling to memories of Daddy. I brought the star to my room after we took down the tree. I intended to return it to the attic, but I stuck it up here at the last minute." She pulled the bright silver ornament out of the box. "Look," she whispered, relief and joy filling her.

"It's beautiful."

"Let's go put it on the tree," she insisted, heading for the door.

"Uh, Lisa, don't you think you should get dressed first, just in case your mother comes home?"

She looked down at herself in surprise. "Maybe you're right. Besides, now that I think about it, it's kind of cold running around without clothes." Her laughter was light-hearted as she began pulling on the clothes they'd hastily tossed on the floor. "Come on. Get dressed. I want you to help me."

Ryan, too, began donning his clothes. In record time, Lisa was pulling him down the stairs to the den. Just as they entered, Margaret's car was heard coming up the drive.

"It's a good thing we got dressed," Ryan murmured.

"Mom will be pleased," Lisa said, ignoring his words. All her thoughts were focused on the star.

When Margaret came in, Lisa and Ryan were standing by the tree, arm in arm, waiting for her. Lisa hurried through the explanation for Ryan's presence to show her mother the star.

"Look! I found it."

"I'm so glad, dear. Are you going to put it on the tree?"

Lisa reached up on tiptoe, but the top of the tree eluded her fingertips. She looked to Ryan for help and he settled the star in its place.

Almost at once, the lights on the tree began blinking, sparkling the tinsel and ornaments. Startled, the three people stared at each other and then around the room, but there were no other signs of electricity.

They looked back at the tree just as the other lights came on in the room and the sound of the central heating system clicked on. Ryan, staring up at the star, muttered, "Must've been a power surge."

Lisa and Margaret looked at each other and linked their arms around Ryan. He might think it was a power surge, but they felt sure it was a Christmas gift from Frank, a blessing for the future, a new memory to savor with the old.

SHARE THE FUN . . .
SHARE YOUR NEW-FOUND TREASURE!!

You don't want to let your new books out of your sight? That's okay. Your friends can get their own. Order below.

No. 25 **LOVE WITH INTEREST** by Darcy Rice
Stephanie & Elliot find $47,000,000 *plus* interest—true love!

No. 26 **NEVER A BRIDE** by Leanne Banks
The last thing Cassie wanted was a relationship. Joshua had other ideas.

No. 28 **SEASON OF THE HEART** by Ann Hammond
Can Lane and Maggie's newfound feelings stand the test of time?

No. 29 **FOSTER LOVE** by Janis Reams Hudson
Morgan comes home to claim his children but Sarah claims his heart.

No. 30 **REMEMBER THE NIGHT** by Sally Falcon
Joanna throws caution to the wind. Is Nathan fantasy or reality?

No. 31 **WINGS OF LOVE** by Linda Windsor
Mac & Kelly soar to new heights of ecstasy. Are they ready?

No. 32 **SWEET LAND OF LIBERTY** by Ellen Kelly
Brock has a secret and Liberty's freedom could be in serious jeopardy!

No. 33 **A TOUCH OF LOVE** by Patricia Hagan
Kelly seeks peace and quiet and finds paradise in Mike's arms.

Meteor Publishing Corporation
Dept. 1192, P. O. Box 41820, Philadelphia, PA 19101-9828

Please send the books I've indicated below. Check or money order (U.S. Dollars only)—no cash, stamps or C.O.D.s (PA residents, add 6% sales tax). I am enclosing $2.95 plus 75¢ handling fee for *each* book ordered.

Total Amount Enclosed: $_____.

___ No. 5	___ No. 15	___ No. 21	___ No. 28
___ No. 27	___ No. 16	___ No. 22	___ No. 29
___ No. 113	___ No. 17	___ No. 23	___ No. 30
___ No. 12	___ No. 18	___ No. 24	___ No. 31
___ No. 13	___ No. 19	___ No. 25	___ No. 32
___ No. 14	___ No. 20	___ No. 26	___ No. 33

Please Print:
Name _____

Address _____ Apt. No. _____

City/State _____ Zip _____

Allow four to six weeks for delivery. Quantities limited.